"Why give me the impression that this is one great big con game?"

"I don't know. Because you have a suspicious nature?"

"You know darn well I have a good reason to be suspicious of you!"

"It's just a mental quirk," he assured her as he bustled into her bedroom and rummaged among her clothes. "This is a nice dress."

"It's a caftan. And, if you think I'm going to let you put that on me, you've got another thing coming, Philip Atmor."

"I can't seem to find a suitable bra."

"Don't you dare!"

EMMA GOLDRICK describes herself as a grandmother first and an author second. She was born and raised in Puerto Rico, where she met her husband, a career military man from Massachusetts. His postings took them all over the world, which often led to mishaps—such as the Christmas they arrived in Germany before their furniture. Emma uses the places she's been as backgrounds for her books, but just in case she runs short of settings, this prolific author and her husband are always making new travel plans.

Books by Emma Goldrick

Don't miss any of our special offers. Write to us at the following address for information on our newest releases.

Harlequin Reader Service
P.O. Box 1397, Buffalo, NY 14240
Canadian address: P.O. Box 603,
Fort Erie, Ont. L2A 5X3

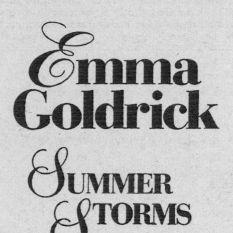

Emma Goldrick

Summer Storms

Harlequin Books

TORONTO • NEW YORK • LONDON
AMSTERDAM • PARIS • SYDNEY • HAMBURG
STOCKHOLM • ATHENS • TOKYO • MILAN
MADRID • WARSAW • BUDAPEST • AUCKLAND

ISBN 0-373-11608-X

SUMMER STORMS

Copyright © 1991 by Emma Goldrick.

This edition published by arrangement with Harlequin Enterprises B. V.

CHAPTER ONE

Ms. CLAUDIA SYLVIA had been secretary to the president of Atmor Fisheries for forty years, starting six years prior to the birth of the present occupant of that chair. So when she heard his voice raised in anger she ducked her head and regretted putting the call through. Young Phil Atmor had a marvelously extended vocabulary, much of it unprintable. And when she heard that familiar ripping sound as he tore the telephone wires from the wall Claudia calmly pulled the cover over her word processor, shoved her "In" basket into the well of her desk for its protection, and stood up, wondering why, after the fights of the last months, she hadn't told Charlotte MacEnnaly to call back some time early in the next century.

But at least she was spared one anguish—he didn't throw the telephone through the window this time. And, with that thought in mind, Claudia Sylvia scuttled out of the office, turned right in the corridor, and ducked into the safety of the janitor's supply cupboard, just in time to hear him storm down the hall yelling at the elevator operator.

"I'll kill that damn woman," Phil Atmor muttered to himself as he settled back in the seat of his new Porsche and sent it roaring out of the garage. "Or maybe that's too good for her.'' He pounded on the steering wheel for emphasis.

A hundred horns blared at him as he forced his way into the traffic flow. The road was slick from the earlier New England summer rain, and there was the smell of fog and salt water from the harbor, not two streets away. Two sea gulls, resting on the superstructure of the old bridge, launched and headed seaward in disgust. A two-tone horn blared from behind him. Phil squirmed around in his seat and glared at the other car. The tires on the vehicle following him squealed as it almost collided with the pier abutment. All of which made Phil feel slightly better. But only slightly.

As he wheeled down onto the Neck he was imagining some of the better tortures. Boiling oil, perhaps? Crucifixion? How in God's name could such a tiny bit of fluff upset his whole ordered life? For two months or more Charlotte MacEnnaly had been a thorn in his side. A world-class concert violinist, no less. Now she had become a carbuncle on his pride. He slowed at the floating bridge that connected Norman's Island to the mainland. It was a temporary structure, erected just after the 1937 hurricane, and the planks bounced and crackled under the car's weight. The selectmen had been guaranteeing its replacement *almost at once*—for the past fifty-odd years. But Norman's Island consisted of only thirty-six acres, barely a hundred yards off shore from the town of Fairhaven, and there were only two houses on the place. The town had higher priorities.

The sun broke through the clouds as he approached the houses. They were Cape Cod cottages, built hardly a hundred yards apart, occupying the top of the slight rise known as the Hill, perhaps fifty feet above the high-water mark. A few scattered and stunted trees shared the open space with the acre or two of grass that surrounded both houses. The rest of the island was nothing but a sand dune, sloping down into the bay. At spring tide, with a full moon, a considerable part of the island would be underwater. On normal days it possessed one of the finest beaches in the state.

As was more than usual these days, a state police car was parked at the edge of the eight-foot-high chain-link fence that marked the boundary between the two properties. The car's red-and-blue roof light revolved wearily. And there he saw, sitting on her front steps, Charlotte MacEnnaly.

"How could you *not* see her?" he grunted to himself as he slammed on his brakes and skidded to a stop on the narrow dirt road. "With all that flaming sunshine sparking over her flaming red hair! I ought to pull it out of her head, one flaming strand at a time." The idea was pleasant. He banged on his steering wheel again, trying his best to swallow his anger.

"After all, I'm a businessman of some repute," he muttered to himself as the whisper of his engine came to a halt. "Why should I let that little monster get into my goody bag?"

"Stodgy businessman," she had said during their last argument. "Pompous! I can tell what mood you're in by the suit you're wearing." He gritted his teeth. He admitted to being perhaps a little conservative, but pompous? No way! Boiling oil was too good for her. Drawn and quartered—that was the answer!

It was such a pleasant thought that he was almost smiling as he climbed out of his car. "Well?"

The patrol officer, cautious despite his size and armament, came over to him. "She says it's your damn pet again."

"*She* says? My *damn* pet?"

"That's what she says. Your pet and her Guarnerius violin."

"Oh, Lord." Phil Atmor wrestled with his anger and shifted down to reality. Her Guarnerius concert violin? Almost as valuable as a Stradivarius. Worth thousands, and irreplaceable in these modern times. The fat would really be in the fire this time! Diplomacy would be required. He shuddered at the thought. "Sam ate the violin?"

"I don't rightly know. You'd better ask her, Mr. Atmor. Gently, please. My lieutenant says that if there are any more riots between you two I should take you both in and lock you up in the same cell."

"A sadist, your lieutenant," Phil grumbled. "Okay, I'll *talk* to her. No reason why I should be frightened off by a five-foot-six-inch redhead, is there?"

"Probably not." The policeman was six feet tall, but still had to look up at Phil. "But I'd be mighty careful about that baseball bat she's packing."

"Oh, Lord. You didn't take it away from her?"

"She doesn't need a license for a baseball bat, and she's on *her* property, Mr. Atmor."

"How can a woman who looks so tasty be so damn inedible?" Phil grumbled. The policeman shrugged his shoulders and leaned back against the side of his patrol car.

Phil Atmor took a moment to pull down his shirt and straighten his tie. My goodness, he lectured himself disgustedly. You made the Federal Fisheries Office back down just six weeks ago; why should you be afraid of—well, all right, concerned about—this little female? He would have preferred to go by his living room to dump a shot of brandy into the well of his courage, but it was too late for that. He squared his shoulders and stepped off smartly until he reached the fence.

"Not another step farther!" She was up and moving forward, the bat held awkwardly in the crook of her arm. Phil stopped and took a deep breath. He could see the tip of the bat swaying in great circles. Obviously Charlie MacEnnaly knew nothing at all about baseball or bats. And, as Phil remembered from his marine corps days, that was exactly the sort of person who knocked you dead—by accident, of course.

He extended one foot beyond the boundary line. The head of her bat centered at about his navel. Despite all his diplomatic intentions, his temper flared. "You called me," he snarled at her. "Here I am. What the hell is the matter this time?"

"Just don't step on my property," she returned with exaggerated slowness. Her husky low voice throbbed. Passion? Anger? Phil pulled his foot back.

Red curly hair, forming a halo around her heart-shaped face. Beautiful pale skin, marked by a string of freckles across the bridge of her nose. The light blue sweater outlined some delightfully gentle curves. Her legs were covered by stirrup pants; they clung lovingly to her well-rounded hips. And all going to waste, Phil told himself. A concert violinist, for crying out loud! She'd make one hell of a good striptease dancer! "Well?" she asked.

"Well what?"

"I told you over the phone," she told him. "Or did you hang up on me again?"

She moved a step or two closer. Her pert little breasts swayed against the slight restriction of her sweater. The movement caught Phil's eyes. Caught and held them. I wonder—? Phil started to ask himself.

"You'll never know, Mr. Atmor," she interrupted his thoughts. Her eyes had followed his, and recognized his target. If it were possible for a well-tanned outdoorsman to blush, Phil Atmor would have done just that. It's all part of her come-on, he told himself fiercely. Get your act together, Atmor!

"Hang up? I wouldn't do a thing like that." Keep the voice under control, that's it. She gave him a chilly unbelieving smile. His self-control slipped.

"Hell, no," he roared. "I didn't hang up. I tore the damn telephone out of the wall."

"Oh, dear, that *is* expensive," she commented. Her sarcasm was spread six feet deep over the statement.

"As long as you're not going to beat each other up I've got another call to answer," the policeman called.

Charlie MacEnnaly waved casually at him with her bat. Phil ducked. The officer chuckled, climbed into his patrol car, and drove off.

"Now, then, to business," she said.

Phil Atmor took three deep breaths. She stared at him as if he were some exercise nut. "Look, Miss Mac-Ennaly—"

"My friends call me Charlie," she interrupted.

"Look—Miss MacEnnaly." He stopped to clear his throat, and then counted to ten, forward and backward. Six deep breaths. He could feel his control returning. She's only a woman, for heaven's sake!

"It may seem inconsequential to you, but I manage to operate a corporation with more than eight hundred employees. Our gross production this last year was almost two hundred million dollars. Surely we— you and I—could come to some understanding? Why don't we step over to my house and let Miss Standish make us a good cup of coffee while we talk things over?"

There was a definite smirk on her face. "Your housekeeper has flown the coop, Mr. Atmor. Around about ten o'clock this morning she brushed Sam out the back door with her broom, and then she called a cab and went off into the wild blue." Those devilish green eyes stabbed at him, looking for a response and finding none. "You don't have much luck with housekeepers, do you? If I count right, that makes three this month!"

He required a good deal of muscular strain to keep from retorting. Counting to ten didn't seem to be enough; he tried the same in German. He could see her hands nervously twisting at the bat.

A thought sprang to mind, one so simple that he wondered how he could have missed it for all this time. If I don't react she'll stop all this nonsense, he told himself. Look at the bloom on her cheeks and the gleam in her eyes. She loves these wild arguments. What a stodgy life she must live if the most fun she gets out of it lies in baiting a neighbor! And I've been a perfect patsy for her for two months or more! Come on, Phil, get control of yourself! Which was an idea more easily thought than practiced.

"Well," she added after the silence, "I hear she wasn't much of a cook anyway." Her lovely little head tilted to one side, the better to watch his face, as she added another dagger thrust. "Although I will admit she was a cute one." He refused to rise to the bait, and in the silence she wound down to a stop. The flush faded from her face, and her freckles dominated. She scuffed one foot in the grass and watched his face carefully.

"Maybe we could go over to *my* house for that coffee?" It was a tentative offer, as if her manners told her she had to make it while her mind told her otherwise.

"Yes, why don't we?" He found it hard to sound enthusiastic, and yet, he told himself, you have to. This flaming feud business has got to stop! You make all kinds of points with the selectmen—why can't you accommodate one young woman?

Charlie turned and ambled across the lawn toward her side door. He followed, admiring her hip movement. Not until they reached the stairs did he remember. "But where's Sam?"

"Your stupid damn pet is in my shed," she stated flatly.

"My *stupid* pet?"

"You heard me. If you let him out you'll be responsible for any further damage he does."

"You bet," he muttered under his breath as he turned and headed for the tool shed behind the house. *My* stupid pet? Old Sam? How old *was* Sam at this very moment? Ten? Eleven? I was twenty-one when Sam was weaned; the only bit of my youth left, Sam. I picked him up at the pet shop right after my mother and father divorced. Right after Emily found out I was broke and gave me the brush-off. Good Lord, Sam must be over thirteen!

He fumbled with the latch on the shed door. Sam heard, and began to grumble. The shed was old, the door was out of line, and the latch was rusted. He struggled with it for a moment, then kicked the bottom of the door. It fell open, and Sam waddled out into the sunshine.

Poor old Sam. As big as a large St. Bernard dog but totally black. He looked to weigh in at eighty pounds. A fair portion of that weight was suspended in his belly. That droop, combined with his short legs, made it difficult for Sam to climb or run. And, to make him even more ridiculous, his tail was only a tiny curl of a thing. His feet were so tiny that it seemed impossible that they could hold up his body. A gentle, affectionate pet, one of the most intelligent of the land-based mammals, big enough to make people cautious, and small enough to be a house pet. His flat snout sniffled constantly, as if he had a permanent cold in his nose.

"C'mon out, boy," he called. His pet pig gave him one delighted grunt, waddled right by him, and rushed out to the front porch, where he tried vainly to jump up on Charlie MacEnnaly, and then gave it up to slobber over her shoe. Phil Atmor shook his head disgustedly and followed. My pet pig, he told himself with a sigh. A miniature black porker with no sense of discrimination. He ate anything, and loved anybody. He was making a desperate effort to climb up the porch step next to his "sweetheart," and wasn't succeeding. Phil leaned over and helped with a shove to Sam's portly posterior. The animal snorted a sort of thanks as his tiny legs began to function.

"My dumb damn pet," he acknowledged wryly as he looked over at Charlie. Her eyes twinkled, and a little smile played at the corners of her mouth. He could not help but return it.

"Oh, I don't know. Maybe he's not as stupid as I had thought. Sometimes he can be very discriminating." She chucked the pig on the back of his neck—or at least where she thought his neck began—and was startled at the soft smoothness of the skin. Sam was making a noise . . . perhaps even purring? Startled at the idea, she gestured toward the door. "Please come in."

It was the first time Phil had ever been in her house. She had been in his twice, both times frothing at the mouth. *His* living room looked as if it were a Spartan barracks. Hers was soft and feminine—and perhaps a little cluttered. It featured a number of plump pillows set in odd corners instead of chairs. On the far side, set under the windows to get the best light, was a baby Steinway piano and a heavy wooden music stand. On top of the piano, glowing in the reflected sunlight, with the patina of centuries on it, was her violin.

Phil took a deep breath as his eye caught the instrument. When he exhaled the air came out in a relieved sigh. She turned to look over her shoulder, following his eye, and she gave him a grim look.

"Not my violin, Mr. Atmor. My case." She waved toward the nearest crimson pillow, where some bits of wreckage lay. "I had it made specially to protect my instrument while traveling. The best leather Europe could provide. We've been around the world twice, that case and I, without a dent. Your pet sat on it, and then began to eat it. Don't you feed the damn animal? And what sensible man would keep a pet pig, I ask you?"

That's all she has to do, Phil thought. Make some thoughtless remark, and his temper would normally be off and away. But today he was trying, really trying, to maintain a good rapport with the woman. "I was lonely," he said. "Even a bachelor tycoon can get lonely. You wouldn't know lonely."

"Don't bet on it," she snapped. "I don't think there's anything more lonely than a concert violinist on tour. Sometimes I've played four different towns in six days. Hey, fella, lonely I know."

He looked at her skeptically. For some reason she was breathing deeply. Her breasts weren't all that small, he thought. Wouldn't this be a fine time to say something like "Lie down here, I want to talk to you"? But he managed to catch his tongue before it ran away with him.

"I was lonely," he repeated. "I'm terribly allergic to cat and dog hair. So I bought a miniature pig. They're easy to house-train, smarter than dogs and cats, clean as can be, and they'll be with you for thirty years or more. Sam and I, we've been together for almost fourteen years. There's always a little trouble, of course. I had to get permission from the Board of Health to keep a pig inside the town limits. That's why I leased the house over here. Now, about this case?"

Her pointing hand indicated the *corpus delicti*. The case looked dead, squashed flat in the middle, nibbled at on both sides, completely ruined. He told her so. She agreed. "I'll pay for the damage, of course," he insisted.

"You'd better believe it," she said sarcastically. When she told him the cost he almost swallowed his tongue. He was one of those businessmen who believed in the Ben Franklin admonition, "A penny saved is two pence clear." Paying for her new violin case was going to cost his personal bank account a pretty penny indeed. He grimaced at his own pun. Once again that little flicker of a smile played at the corners of her mouth. He stepped over to the piano and checked the sheet music on the stand. "Violin Concerto in D Major," by Peter Tchaikovsky. He commented vaguely.

"Oh? You're familiar with classical music?" It seemed a shame to dampen that smile. Phil's idea of good music usually ran from jazz to country, centered around Willie Nelson, the Dixieland Band and Dolly Parton. He wasn't really sure how to pronounce this fellow Tchaikovsky's name. All of his extensive education had dealt narrowly with money-making. Economics, they called it at Harvard. "A lovely piece of work," he muttered.

"Yes," she said. "I need a tune-up before my next tour so I've arranged to play the concerto with the Boston Symphony in two weeks. Shall we have coffee in the kitchen?"

"I hadn't realized that concert violining was such an expensive hobby," he commented as he followed that wonderful swaying posterior into the kitchen. He took quick note. Her dining room, next to the kitchen, had been converted into a bedroom. Perhaps she hated to use the upstairs? Charlie gestured to a chair as she went by him toward the gas stove and the coffeepot.

"It's not a hobby. It's my living." For a moment she looked indignant, then her face relaxed into that cautious smile again, a sort of "well, what can he possibly know?" expression. "I slaved for fifteen years to acquire what skill I have," she added. "Do you play, Mr. Atmor?"

"Phil, please. Call me Phil." Yes, I play, he told himself. Poker, parlor games... How could I have lived this long and not done something about my education? The woman's giving me an inferiority complex!

Silence. The pot boiled. She moved to get two mugs down from the cupboard, and set them on the table. "Black?"

"Black," he acknowledged. There seemed to be something more to be said. Something conciliatory. "I've heard you play from next door—er—Charlie. It's not half bad."

Her smile faded. She glared at him across the big round kitchen table. Now what did I say? he asked himself. Not half bad? Talk about damning with faint praise! "I didn't mean that exactly the way it sounded," he offered humbly. "You play excellently. I've heard you practicing while I'm at breakfast, and again while I'm at supper, and I—hey, I'm not complaining, mind you..."

The little smile came back, and turned into a gamine grin. "But yes, you are, aren't you, Mr. Atmor?" She leaned back in her captain's chair and ran her fingers through her marvelous hair. "It takes practice. I do two hours in the morning, and two in the afternoon."

"Seven days a week?"

"Oh, sometimes I take Sunday afternoon off," she admitted. "Especially in the football season."

There's common ground, he told himself. Jump on it quickly. "Ah, you're a football fan?"

"I hate it," she returned. The smile vanished. "But you—you like football. And you play that damn television set so loudly that they can hear it over on the mainland and I can't hear myself practice! Sometimes I wish I had taken up drums."

His promise to reform was caught off base. She received his normal reaction. "Well, if I don't play it loudly I can't hear what's going on over that damn fiddle playing," he growled.

Charlie MacEnnaly got slowly up to her feet. Her face had turned red again, and there was a twitch under her eye. Phil watched cautiously. There was no telling what she might do, that one, and she had a half cup of hot coffee in her hand.

"Fiddling?" Her voice had risen from a pleasant alto to a glacial soprano. "Fiddle playing?"

Did it again, he told himself. "Isn't that what they call it?"

She crossed her arms over her breasts and seemed to be adding up lists of his worst failings. "Your damn pig dug up all my petunias yesterday," she cataloged in a flat monotone. "And every time I start to practice he runs over beneath my window and grunts and whistles and moans at me!"

"I don't know why," he retorted. His own control was fluttering away on the May wind that was stirring the kitchen curtains. "I suppose he loves you. He's not really a great music lover."

"Damn you, Philip Atmor! Just what the devil do you mean by that?" She was edging slowly around the table, getting just a little too close for comfort, and Phil couldn't remember where she had put the baseball bat.

"Nothing. Nothing particularly," he said. "One of the reasons I took the house next door was so I could have some peace and quiet. Last year it was great."

"And then I came along? I'm to blame for all this?"

"You said it, not me."

"It would be simpler if you'd keep your darn pig on a leash," she stated.

"On a leash?" He held up both hands heaven-ward. Charlie looked down at the adoring pig, stand-ing just behind him. The animal wore a collar, but it was purely decorative. If Sam had once had a neck, it had been a long time ago. Now his head seemed to be stapled directly onto his shoulders!

"It might help too if you would cut down on those wild parties," she added. As she talked the list of his sins grew longer. "Or at least stop the damn orgies out on the front lawn!"

"Orgies? What the hell do you mean, *orgies*?"

"An old-fashioned term," she yelled back at him, "for when two women and a man, all three naked, are rolling around in the grass—which you never seem to cut, Mr. Atmor—and singing lewd songs at the top of their voices!"

"Nobody I ever invited would act like that," he re-torted as he mentally scanned his list of party friends and decided to prune some names from his list. "And you're not Miss Perfect Neighbor, either, lady. How about waiting until Sunday morning before you bring in your crew to put up that chain-link fence? Sunday—the only day I keep free for sleeping in!"

"It's not my fault that the only contractor avail-able in a hurry could only work on the weekend," she huffed. "I wouldn't have needed the fence if your damn pet pig didn't keep wandering over to *my* prop-erty to do his business! And if you had sent your girlfriend home on that Saturday night you wouldn't have been so embarrassed!"

"Embarrassed? I'll show you embarrassed," he told her as she backed away from him. And then another thought struck. "By heaven, you're jealous." He roared with laughter. "No need for that, lady. I admit that you're not right up there with the top beauties of the day. But with a brown paper bag over your head you'd be quite the thing. Any time you feel like sharing, just come on over and I'll put your name on my list."

"Why you—you damnable insulting prig," she muttered. "I'd like to—"

Whatever it was that she would like to was not to be discovered, for that was the moment when Sam, tired of the long discussion, came up behind Phil, stretched upward on his hind legs and sent him catapulting into Charlie.

There was only one way to keep them both from banging off the wall. He wrapped the girl up in his arms and held on for dear life, pressing her head hard against his chest, locking her arms down at her sides, and smothering whatever it was she was trying to say against his shirt. He also whirled them both around so that he took the brunt of the punishment when they slammed into the kitchen sink.

Good turn Phil, he told himself, here's where I get my reward. He bounced back off the sink with her still locked in his arms. For some reason he just didn't feel like releasing her, even though his back was aching. She squirmed against him, and it added a wonderful feeling to the mix. Soft, sweet-smelling, altogether delightful. He dipped his square chin into the mass of her curls. They teased him. His worst enemy, and he was kissing the top of her head—and enjoying it. The more she squirmed, the better he liked it.

My worst enemy, he repeated, and then looked over the top of her head to where Sam was giving him irritated looks. That was enough to bring him back to attention. Push her away, he told himself. But at this close angle he could see how truly angry she was. Her fists were clenched as she tried to break free. Push her away—carefully—he told himself. It wasn't the easiest job in the world, but she was truly a *little* girl; a raging angry little girl.

By this time there was space between them as his hands locked on her wrists to protect himself from the slashing fingernails. Like a wrestler trying to make a clean break, he finally forced her back another step or two, and then slowly released her, one wrist at a time.

She stood there, face flushed, almost gibbering, trembling so badly that she shook from head to toe.

"Sorry about that," he muttered as he watched warily. "Sam—"

"That's right. Blame it on the pig." She swallowed hard and relaxed her fists. He could see the marks of her fingernails in her palms. Perspiration glistened on her forehead. "Compared to you, Mr. Atmor, Sam is a perfect gentleman!"

"Look, it was a mistake," he protested. "An accident. Sam came up behind me, and—no! Sam!"

The pig had done it again, but this time he had moved around behind Charlie before he jumped, and she was thrown forward into Phil's arms again. He could see the startled look in her green eyes, and knew vaguely that he was in more trouble than he could stand. But then, being already in over his head, he told himself, he might as well go the whole hog.

The woman seemed to be paralyzed, staring up at him as if unable to move or speak. She moistened her dry lips with a nervous tongue, and he knew that, given a chance, she'd rip him up one side and down the other. There was only one way to shut her off at the source. He lowered his head and sealed her lips with his own.

He had meant it to be a simple expedient, a way to keep her quiet, and for that first second she seemed frozen, but after that she melted, her lips parted, and the expedient kiss got away from Phil and turned into an adventure he had not expected. Willingly he followed the feeling, exploring the softness of her mouth, loosening one hand to stroke her soft back, pulling her closer until she was standing on her toes.

Phil Atmor had kissed more than his share of females in a life devoted to the sport, but this was the first time he had been caught up in his own backwash. If it were not for the shortage of breath he might have continued for hours. But breathing was as necessary a function as was kissing. He gently released the pressure of his arms and she settled to the floor, her eyes covered with a glassy film, half closed. Phil took one step back, and cleared his throat.

Her eyes opened wide. She seemed as if she were recovering consciousness after being in a deep dream. She looked around the room vaguely, and then her mouth tightened, and he could see her right arm flexing.

"No," he cautioned. "Your fingers are your fortune, lady. Don't!"

"Dirty... rotten..." she muttered.

"Don't," Phil warned, alarmed, not at what she could do to him, but what she might do to herself. But Charlie MacEnnaly was far beyond thought or logic. In the white heat of her Highland ancestors, she wound up like a major league pitcher and swung her open right hand at his chin with all the force of her tiny body behind it. He drew his head back. Her palm missed the target, but as it went by his rocky chin her fingers were caught and bent backward. There was so much force in her blow that even with this near miss Phil was rocked back on his heels. But Charlie was bent over in front of him, treasuring her right hand within her left, crying.

"Get out of here," she moaned.

"You need help."

"Not yours. Just get out. I'm sure anything you touch would infect me. Get out!"

"Okay," he yelled at her. "I get the message. Bubonic plague, that's me?"

"Or worse," she muttered.

For a moment Phil had trouble moving his feet, then, muttering a curse under his breath, he turned around and stalked to the door. Sam, caught between two emotions, finally clung to the older love, and followed him. The pair of them were hardly out of the door when Charlie groaned. Phil turned around to look.

She was crumpled up in her chair, one hand holding the other, and tears were falling silently down her cheeks. "That's it," Phil declared. "That is surer than Satan all there is." He stomped across the floor and plucked her out of the chair as if she were paper-weight.

"What—what are you doing?" she gasped at him.

"I'm taking you to St. Luke's Hospital," he said. Looking down at her, he could see that her lovely little face had collapsed; tears were flowing in abundance, although she made not a sound. Even her lush red hair seemed to straggle.

"I—don't want a hospital," she whispered. "Put me down."

"Just for once in your young life, shut up," he said. "You're about to be done good to, and I'm the doer." He could feel her stiffen in his arms, and then relax completely. They headed for the door, Sam trailing, and out to his car. With infinite care he installed her in the front seat, fastened her seat belt, and used his car rug to build her a support for the injured hand and arm. Sam, already in the back seat, stuck his snout in between the seats and watched intently.

"We'll go slow and easy," Phil told Charlie. She made a noise, a sort of agreement. They went over the bridge at five miles an hour, but as they proceeded up the Neck the speed gradually increased. He drove across Route 6, looking for the superhighway. And when their wheels were on Route 195 he turned the Porsche loose. They pulled in under the shelter of the roofed entrance to the emergency room a full four minutes ahead of the two patrol cars that had been chasing them. After Phil came back out, having made all the arrangements for Charlie's treatment, he unveiled his most innocent expression and tried to talk himself out of a traffic ticket.

"I don't know what happened," Phil told Sam when the officers, not quite satisfied, drove off. The pig settled down on the back seat, laying his massive head close to the window, and looking up at him with a disgusted look on his face.

"But then," Phil said, "you look disgusted half the time anyway. Look, Sam. It wasn't my fault!" He moved his car away from the emergency entrance, and parked in the no-parking space a few feet away. "It wasn't my fault, Sam!" His pig looked at him in sad disbelief and rolled over before he went to sleep. He didn't wake up until Charlotte came walking unsteadily out of the clinic.

On her right hand and lower arm she wore a big white cast.

"Charlie?" Phil sounded as if he had just heard the trumpet of doom. "Good Lord, Charlie, what can I do—?"

"You've done enough for me already," she said softly. "Just drive me home—please."

"But what...?"

She settled back in the corner. "Look," she said, sighing. "You broke my little finger. You bruised the others. And you sprained my wrist. You have succeeded completely in ruining my livelihood. Isn't that enough for one day? Just put it on your score card and take me home. I need to get to bed. Maybe I could sleep the night out and wake up tomorrow to find that you've moved to east Berlin."

"You should live in hope," he muttered. Charlie gave him a disgusted look and closed her eyes. Sam grunted at him and added a scowl. When even your pig is mad at you, Phil thought, you're in a terrible position. He started the car and drove soberly all the way back to Norman's Island.

CHAPTER TWO

CHARLOTTE MACENNALY had trouble sleeping that night. Her hand ached. The anesthetic administered in the clinic while they had set the bones in her finger was wearing off. There were plenty of painkillers in her prescription bottle, but she was too impatient, too angry to use them immediately. She put out all the lights in her own house, drew back the living room curtains, and watched the lights across the yard.

What do you suppose Phil's doing now? she asked herself. Whatever it is, I hope it hurts. Look at that. My bow hand. I won't be able to play for—good Lord, I'll have to cancel the Boston recital. And I won't be able to practice for weeks! And all *his* fault. Him and that—Sam. It's what you get for living such a narrow life, Charlie MacEnnaly. When you come out into the wide, wide world you get your hand broken!

All those years I've put into this infernal grind. Did I really *want* to be a musician? If so, why do all the critics keep saying that I play with technical perfection, but still list me in the second tier? Critics! What the devil do *they* know? She cradled her aching hand in the palm of the other as she paced back and forth in front of the window.

Maybe he did me a favor, breaking my hand! It gives me a chance to think. And with that settled she turned back to the window. There was a bright three-quarter moon outside, painting the sand silver. She could hear the hoot of a hunting owl over on the mainland. Up against her fence there was a flash of movement. Rabbits. The island was infested with them.

But her thoughts kept coming back to the house next door. If he's having such a good time over there, why don't I hear some noise? Usually there's an up-roar, and tonight everything is so quiet that I can hear the waves splashing up on the beach.

But why should *I* care about what he says or thinks or does? He's only a man, good for one thing only, and I don't need *that*! Or him. A tall skinny bean-pole, he is. I've seen better-looking men on the backs of baseball cards. Well, perhaps he isn't all *that* skinny. And so darn tall! I don't believe I've seen a man that tall since they introduced me to those bas-ketball players. Where was that? Italy? France? I've traveled so darn much that I can't remember the dif-ference between one country and another. And *he* thinks he knows lonely!

Strong. I'll give him that. Three times a week he brings out that zinc tub and fills it up and then has to wrestle Sam into the water for a bath. No mean feat. Charlie giggled at the remembrance. And when those dark eyes of his glare at you it's soul-chilling. How can a man who acts so fierce have dark curly hair like that? It isn't fair! Pompous stick-in-the-mud!

There finally came a noise from next door. His back door was closing. Sam was being turned out for his nightly constitutional. She could see the little monster as he trotted deliberately around the end of her fence, heading straight for her side door.

Charlie moved back from the window and held her breath. The door still would not latch properly. "Tomorrow," she muttered. "I'll get it fixed tomorrow." In the meantime Sam disappeared from sight due to the angle of the windows. But she heard noises in the dark shadows at the edge of the house.

Two or three preliminary thumps. A pause as if the pig was gathering all his weight and strength. And then a crash as the latch slipped, the door swung open and Sam sauntered into the room. He came directly to her feet as if he had perfect night vision, and nuzzled her bare toe.

"Too much!" She chuckled as she leaned over to scratch his snout. "Now shoo, boy. Go home!" But as far as Sam was concerned he was already home. He headed straight for her bedroom, grunted a couple of times as he measured the comfort of the throw rug at the foot of her bed, and then settled down. Charlie shook her head in disbelief, closed the door, and went into the kitchen to swallow her prescribed two paracetomol.

Charlie was already feeling the effect of the drug by the time she reached the bedroom. She fell onto the brass bed, one of her arms hanging off the side. Vaguely she heard Sam get up and come around to the head of the bed. In another moment she felt the coolness as he licked her fingers before he settled down again.

"That's what I need," she muttered. "A pet. Mr. Uppity's allergic to cats. I'll get me a cat and..." Whatever it was she planned to do slipped her mind as she blanked out. She heard nothing more until someone began thundering on her door, and the morning sun shone directly into her eyes.

Her door was hanging half open when Phil came looking for Sam the next morning. He knocked gently a couple of times but got no answer except for Sam's normal snore. He walked in, moving softly. The girl was lying flat on her back on top of the covers, with her nightgown hiked just above her knees. Lovely woman, he told himself. I wonder who supports her? The girl moved slightly.

"What have you done with my pet?" Phil asked in his normal bass voice. He had been raised in a tough wild business, commercial fishing, and even his normal voice tended to be just short of a roar. Charlie struggled to get one eye open. That rotten—man... had broken into her house, and was yelling at her as if she were a major criminal. And now he was bursting into her *bedroom*!

Charlotte took a deep breath. She had forgotten that she had gone to bed wearing her normal nightwear. In this case, a man's T-shirt, labeled "Property of the Boston Celtics." It fitted too firmly at the top and not at all below mid-thigh. And she was lying *on top* of the blankets, so there was no way she could pull them up over her.

"What are you doing in my bedroom?" she roared back. For a small girl she had a remarkably loud voice.

He seemed taken aback for just a second, and then returned to the attack. "Where's Sam, you damn—pignapper? Just because you don't like pigs there's no need to take out all your aggressions on Sam."

"Oh, I like porkers a great deal," she returned sweetly. "I love pork spare ribs, smoked shoulders, and—especially hams!"

Phil Atmor began to swell up, as if someone were pumping air into him. And then he shook his head and gave a gusty sigh. "Look," he said in a reasoning voice, "I love my pig. What is this? A ransom demand? I'm willing to pay any nominal amount. Name your price."

"You couldn't afford my price, Mr. Atmor," she replied. She had been using her one good hand ineffectively, trying to cover her naked thighs. Now she lifted her right hand and pointed it at him. The cast glistened pure white in the early-morning sun. "Look at that hand. I'm going to sue, Mr. Philip Atmor. Probably for more than six million dollars. Look what you did to me! I can't play a note. I may never be able to play a note again. And for that you're going to pay!"

"Yeah, of course I am." He came to the side of the bed, almost stepping on his pet as he did so. Sam grunted in annoyance and moved out of the way. "Look, lady, you hit me of your own free will. You plan to sue, do you, because I didn't move my face out of the way when you swung your hand? Bull." And then a look at the floor. "Oh, hi, Sam. Good pig. Go along home now and get your breakfast." Sam grunted as if he understood, and waddled out into the living room.

Charlie came back to the fray. "What you fail to remember, Mr. Atmor, is that you were attacking me and I hit you in self-defense."

"I didn't attack. I was pushed."

"By whom? Sam?"

"Exactly. Sam pushed me."

"That'll make a great story in court," she mused. "'Tycoon pushed into molestation by rampant pig.' They'll love that on Wall Street."

Evidently the thought had never occurred to him. Charlie stifled a giggle as a look of surprise ran across his face. You have been lying to yourself, she thought. He may not be handsome, but he is—manly, if there is such a word. On the other hand, how can you respect a man who rushes in to rescue his beloved pet, but not before he dresses, complete with tie and navy blue three-piece suit?

"Burn the suit," she advised, and then clapped a hand over her mouth before any more nonsense could leak out.

Those dark eyes turned on her and seemed to refocus. "Burn the suit?"

"I said get your pig out of here, before I really lose my temper!"

"I could have sworn..." He looked down at himself, and fingered the material of his suit jacket. "Is there something wrong with my suit?"

A hopeless case, Charlie thought. But there's no sense in pursuing the argument. Why do I care that he would look a handsome devil in a pair of jeans and a sports shirt—with the wind ruffling his hair? I wonder if he sails? She might have let something more slip, but by that time he had turned on his heel and stalked out of the house. She could hear him talking to his pet as he slammed her door behind them.

So bad luck to him, Charlie thought as she struggled up out of bed. The pain in her hand had become a dull throb every time she moved the arm. Probably the old Scottish curse was worth less than nothing, but it couldn't hurt. But no curses on his pig; a pig was, after all, a wise and noble beast.

She itched. Last night was the first time since she'd become an adult that she hadn't showered at night. She wandered into the bathroom, but no amount of wiggling could allow her to wash herself without washing the cast. Back to the bedroom. Her troubles seemed to magnify; she could neither get out of her nightgown, or get into her robe. All because she was a strongly right-handed person, and her right hand was useless. She was sitting on the edge of her bed, dejected, when her side door banged open again.

"You again," she snarled.

"Well, look." Charlie could tell by the tone of Phil's voice that he was going to ask for something, no matter how much it embarrassed him.

"So I'm looking."

He winced at the sarcasm with which her statement was loaded. "I have to get to work, Charlie. Now that my housekeeper is gone I need someone to look after Sam while I'm away."

"Sure, leave him with me," she retorted. "I'll call the guy at the slaughterhouse and see if we can't make something useful out of him. As you know, I'm partial to spare ribs."

"Hey! That's no way to talk! He's my pet!"

"He's a pig, damn it. A big, old, ugly pig!"

He drew himself up to full height. Look at that, she told herself. He's changed clothes. Still a three-piece suit, but dark brown, this one, with a pansy yellow necktie. Dear Lord! "You could take him with you," she suggested.

"No, I can't do that." He sighed as if all the world's troubles were on his shoulders. "I—my company has just helped to rebuild the Boy Scout camp out at Miles Standish Forest Reservation. I promised I'd be there for the opening ceremony."

"You could send an assistant vice president," she suggested. Her left hand was busily scratching at her right shoulder. There was a place there, right out of reach, that was driving her crazy.

"No, I couldn't. If it were the mayor, or something like that, I would. But I promised the kids I'd come. If we're to make this a better world to live in we must always keep our word to the kids!"

Not fair, Charlie thought! Just when I get him classified as a certifiable idiot he tells me something with which I absolutely have to agree! Totally unfair! It had to be challenged to reveal him in his normal prissiness.

"Bet you made a fortune out of *that* contract," she snapped. He cocked his head and an unbelieving expression ran across his face and was gone.

"This is what is called *pro bono* work," he said softly. "We do something like this twice a year, sometimes more often, to show our appreciation to the community in which we live." A little smile played at his lips, a challenging sort of smile that dared her to make another stupid remark. It left her wordless, an unusual position for a member of the MacEnnaly family, and in the meantime he progressed from victory to victory.

"Your shoulder itches?" And before Charlie could rally an insulting answer, his big paw had replaced hers. "There?"

"A little farther back," she muttered. "Just a smidgen to the left. Aaaaaah!"

"What you need is a good hot shower."

Charlie was determined not to go down in defeat. "Sure I do," she muttered bitterly. "How the devil do you think I can shower without getting this cast wet?"

"No problem." His hand wrapped itself around her left elbow. She came up off the bed as if shot from a cannon, all without a bit of help from her own muscles.

"Dear Lord," she gasped.

He smiled down at her. "Bathroom in the same place as mine?" Charlie nodded her head. Her feet had a hard time keeping up with her upper body as he whisked her out of the bedroom and into the bathroom.

"Not bad. Your tiles are brighter than mine."

She wanted very badly to tell him it was because she polished hers daily, while his parade of housekeepers all believed in a swipe and a prayer, but the words would not come.

"Now, sit right here." That well-muscled arm guided her to a perch on the rail of the tub. "Be right back."

Sure you will, she told herself dazedly as she watched his back. I'll wait. I don't have anything to do until six weeks from Tuesday. I'll just sit right here and—

But he was back in a minute, carrying one of her plastic garbage bags. And the biggest surprise—he had taken off his jacket and shirt! "Hold your arm out," he said gently.

"Yes." She had to struggle to keep from squeaking.

"Not that one. The other one." She snatched a quick look, expecting a brittle laugh, but found, instead, a compassionate gleam in those dark eyes. The idea of compassion startled her.

"The other one?" Her right arm came up slowly. You're acting like a retarded child, she lectured herself. And he's so solemn. I wonder if he ever really smiles? What now, mighty male?

He *did* smile, almost as if he had heard her thought. Not a terribly big smile. In fact, it encompassed only half of his mouth, but it was definitely a smile. And while she watched he thrust her damaged hand into the garbage bag, then fastened it all together by wrapping it on with an elastic bandage. "Now," he added, "all you have to do is keep the arm up while you're under the shower, so that nothing leaks. Simple?"

"Yeah. Simple," she muttered. But by that time his back was to her as he turned on both the hot and cold faucets, and carefully tested for the right temperature.

"And there we go." He pulled back the shower curtain and bowed her into the tub.

"Sure," she muttered as she struggled to her feet. "But I hardly ever take a shower with my nightgown on. And I can't get it off one-handed."

"Oh, is that what it is? Your nightgown? I thought it might be a T-shirt of your brother's."

"I don't have a brother."

"Ah. Your last lover?"

"Drop dead," she snarled. He was making altogether too many observations and assumptions, and she was so mentally off-balance that her usually sarcastic wit provided no shield. "What are you—?"

"I'm helping," he said. And he chuckled. It was the first time she had ever heard him sound a note of pleasure. True, it sounded rusty, as if long disused, but it *was* a chuckle. "Duck your head."

And, without thinking, she did, leaving him with most of her nightgown in his hands as he gently worked it down her right arm and over both cast and plastic. Leaving her, her mind finally grasped, totally naked. "What *are* you doing?" she roared.

"Helping." And again that dry chuckle. Try as she might, there was no way she could cover all her frontage with two hands. "Lovely," he commented, and she could swear he was smacking his lips. "Into the shower, my dear." That big hand again on her left elbow. She lifted one foot up; he seemed to provide lifting power for the other. The warm water touched her in welcome; he closed the shower curtain behind her, and said, "How's that?"

"That's fine," she managed. Very weakly said. Here I am, she told herself, trapped inside a shower, totally naked, with a perfect stranger standing outside waiting. Well, perhaps not a *perfect* stranger. And some time or another I have to get out. Time to compromise.

"Thank you." A little louder, but with a slight quaver to her voice. "I've decided I'll baby-sit Sam for you. Why don't you go ahead to your ceremony?"

"Well, that's very neighborly of you," he said. "I'll go get Sam. He'll love this."

"I'll bet he will," she muttered, but there was no answer. Taking a chance, she peeped out, barely moving the curtains enough to let one eye observe. He had gone. "Damn voyeur," she shouted. The noise of the shower drowned out the words. Not in years had any man upset the quiet downstream drift of her life. Not in years? Never! Confused, holding her right hand up, she soaped her left and began to massage her pert, proud breasts. She hardly noticed how the rosy tips of those breasts had hardened.

Phil Atmor came back to the office at about four o'clock, wearing jeans and a bush jacket smeared in various places, with a big smile on his face. "You had a good time at the ceremony, did you?" Claudia Sylvia, his secretary, met him at the door. "And behaved yourself like a gentlemanly businessman?"

"Come off it, Claudia." He brushed at his jacket without much success while she walked around him, pausing to pluck a twig and some leaves from his hair. "So I gave them my best speech, and then we had a great time. Since I had the van, I brought a couple of troops back with me and took them on a harbor cruise on the *Mary and Evelyn*. A good time was had by all."

He dropped into the chair behind his desk and began to pull his vest out of his pants.

"Something wrong, Philip?"

"Not really. Just something I've been thinking of for a couple of weeks. Captain Hardy has had it at sea. His arthritis is killing him. Has he come up yet?"

"Not yet," Claudia said mournfully. "You're not going to let him go?"

"After forty years at sea for Atmor? Never happen!"

"Well, here he is now. Captain Hardy! How are you?"

"All the better for seein' you, young lady. Mr. Atmor, you wanted to see me?"

"Come off it, Captain. Mr. Atmor was my grandfather. Call me Phil. Take a seat. I have some good news for you."

"Good news? I've worried myself all the way up here!"

"I'm sorry for that," Phil said. "To tell the truth, I wasn't sure how you'd take the news. Look, all last week I found myself down in operations trying to tell skippers with more than a hundred trips under their belt what they should do. And me with less than ten trips. That's nonsense, Captain Hardy, don't you agree?"

"Can't say I ever gave it a thought," the old man mused.

"Well, I did," Phil said, chuckling. "I'm losing my playboy image, and our fish landings are going down. So, I figured, why don't I get the most experienced skipper in the fleet, and set him up as director of operations?"

Captain Hardy rubbed the side of his red nose. "You was thinkin' perhaps of me? Shore duty?"

"Yup. There's always some sacrifice to be made. And a thirty percent increase in salary."

"Me?"

"Yup. You. I talked to Millie about it, and she thinks it's great."

"You talked to my wife about it?"

"That's the way I always do business," Phil said. "Always talk to the top brass first."

"You young scallywag," the old man said, chuckling. "Ain't no ways to argue that. When do I start?"

"Monday morning, Commodore. Take the weekend off."

"Philip Atmor," Claudia said softly as the old man walked out jauntily, "you get more slippery every week that goes by. You need a commodore about as much as I need a buggy whip. What's happened to that hard heart?"

"Nothing. Nothing at all." His face was beet red. "And I do need a commodore."

"Yeah, sure. Have you met some girl, Philip?"

His face turned even more red. "Me? A girl? What would I want with a girl?"

His secretary grinned at him. "What indeed?" she said. "Go get yourself a shower!"

He went, whistling, and missed the gleam in his secretary's eye. A motherly gleam. He walked back fifteen minutes later, wearing jeans and an open shirt, his black curly hair sparkling.

"Anything important in the mail?"

"I don't know about important," she said carefully. "But there is a letter marked 'personal.' I think it might be from your mother."

He had been pacing back and forth at the double windows. Now he stopped in midstride. "From my mother? Good Lord, what do you suppose *she* wants?" He held out his hand for the envelope.

Claudia slit the envelope and passed it to him without opening it. He took hardly a moment to read it, muttered something under his breath, and threw the crumpled correspondence into the wastebasket.

"Something serious?" Claudia asked.

"No," he answered abruptly. "Well, maybe yes. She wants to come and see me, and bring a friend along with her."

"Somebody we know?"

"She didn't say, and I'm damned if I'm going to worry about it."

"Never do today what you can put off until tomorrow?"

"Always a smartie, woman." He swooped on her and swung her around in a circle. She shrieked—halfway between laughter and panic.

"Put me down, you . . . you—"

"Monster," he interrupted. But he did put her down. "Everybody seems to be calling me that lately. I don't suppose she called?"

"She who?"

"You know who! Dammit woman, don't get coy with me." His sparkling eyes belied the words.

"Don't you cuss at me," Claudia laughed. "Remember, I used to change your diapers when you were young. And no, she didn't call."

"Damn!" For months he had dreaded those calls from Charlie MacEnnaly, and now he was in a fret because she hadn't called. But of course it was only a minor glitch, he told himself. By tomorrow—hell, by tonight—we'll be back in our usual "hate" mode, and things will be back to normal on Norman's Island. And in the meantime he had had a great excursion, a fine run with the boys, and a lovely afternoon. But then, kids were easier to love than adults.

A memory snatched at him; the sound of that deadly smack when her fingers had struck his chin and she'd bent over in agony. He nibbled at his lower lip and pounded one hand into the other, hoping to drive out the memory, the sense of guilt that enveloped him. So why am I guilty? She hit *me*, not vice versa. Yeah, but . . . His conscience tried to argue with him, to no avail. I'm pompous and she hit me, and she's—good Lord, that woman is beautifully obnoxious!

" 'Burn that suit,' " he muttered, looking down at his jeans. " 'Stodgy,' " he added reflectively.

Claudia moved back a step or two and studied the frown that ruined his looks. No, not handsome, my little boy, she thought. Such a cute baby he had been, and nobody to love him. What a shame. He had grown up too fast, taken on responsibilities too early. He had been barely twenty-two when his father had—died. "Stodgy? Whoever told you that?"

"Oh—just someone I met."

"Perhaps—just the tiniest bit," she agreed. "No more than the normal New England male, believe me."

His smile erased the wrinkles. "And of course you'd know all about New England males, Claudia?"

She was too old to blush. In fact, in its own way, it was a compliment. She took it so, returned his smile, added a roguish wink to it all, and said, "Now, do we get down to business?"

"Anything terribly important?"

"Not really. Mr. Anderson has some trouble in the Plymouth cannery, and he—"

"He's the superintendent," Phil interrupted with a causal wave of his hand. "So let him fix it."

"Ah—is this where we begin the hands-off management that you keep promising me?"

"This is it. I need time to smell the roses. I didn't realize until today how *much* I need that. Can I ask you a couple of questions, Claudia?"

"Ask away." She moved out in front of her own desk and perched on its corner, scanning his face for signs. Who is it? she asked herself. This woman who evidently has caught up with the fastest bachelor in the East? Claudia Sylvia mustered her best "confide in me" expression, and waited. With the first question he staggered her out of her complacent mode.

"Why is it you never married?"

"Me? Married?"

"Come on now, it's important. You've been mothering me for a long time, and I haven't anyone else to ask."

"I—suppose there were a number of reasons," she began slowly.

"Never met the right man?"

Oh, Lord, Claudia sighed to herself. Don't pry at that sore. It's been healed for years. Or at least I think it has. "Oh, I met the right man," she said, doing her best to sound cheerful about that long-gone affair. If it hadn't all come unstuck, I could have been your real mother, Phil Atmor. And I would have named you Peter, not Philip. I hate that "Philip" business.

"So what happened?"

"Nothing unusual, Philip. I met the right man, but a little too late. Some other woman had already met him before I did." Even forced cheerfulness could not continue.

"And you couldn't take any *other* man?"

"Nobody really wants second-best, my dear. Why do you ask?"

"Because—well, I don't really know." He shook his head. His hair was still wet, and water droplets scattered on to the dull green carpet. "Don't get me wrong. I've met lots of girls, but I've never come to *know* one of them. Does that sound stupid?"

"Not a bit. It sounds very, very normal. What's her name?"

"Name?" He *could* blush, and did. "I haven't come to that part yet. Not as far as selecting one woman with a real name, and all that. Besides, for the past couple of months I've been in this running feud with the girl next door."

"She sounds interesting," Claudia teased.

"Interesting! My goodness, the woman's a damn threat to the world. Her and that stupid fiddle of hers. And picky! My parties are too loud, or too long, or Sam is always getting into something at her place. You'd think that she was set down on earth to be my personal devil! I'd like to wring her little neck, believe me!"

There was a moment of silence, and then he continued. "What am I going to do about Charlie MacEnnaly?"

"Charlie MacEnnaly. That's the girl you're feuding with?"

"The very one." He produced a small sigh and a sad shake of the head. "Barely over five feet six, red hair, a nice figure—not overdoing it, but nice—and a parade of freckles across her nose. And a temper big enough for King Kong!"

"She does sound terrifying." His secretary was having a hard time keeping from laughing out loud, but his eyes were on the carpet again as he scuffed at it with one toe, disturbing the mirrorlike shine on his shoes.

"Enough to scare half the world," he agreed. "What I really need to do is teach her a good lesson. Any ideas?"

"You can't stand her?"

"Not a bit."

"And she can't stand you?"

"Not a bit. And yet Sam thinks she's great, and I've never known Sam to make a mistake about people. Never! Well?"

"It's hard to say," Claudia said. "You don't want something simple, like poisoning her well?"

"Too easy. I did think about buying up her house lease, but that's too hard to handle these days."

"Then there's only one way to punish her. One way to give it to her and make it hurt for years." His head snapped up.

"I knew I could depend on you, Claudia. Thank goodness. What's the program?"

Yes, thank goodness for me, Claudia told herself. Wait until I tell him my doctor says I must retire within the year. That'll really throw the cat among the pigeons. And so will this.

"If everything you say is true, Philip, the only way you can really punish this foolish woman is to marry her!"

There was a giggle of laughter from the outer office, where Alice Sturdevent did typing and filing and gossiping and "gofering." Claudia Sylvia shook her head as she walked over and closed the inner door.

"Marry her?" Claudia could see the fiendish grin spread across his face. "Lord, that *would* teach her a lesson, wouldn't it? But—I hadn't meant to get married much before I was forty."

"Well, you can't have everything," Claudia agreed, as she turned her back to him and shuffled papers to no purpose.

CHAPTER THREE

THE rain came just as Phil left the underground garage and started for home. Just a sprinkle at first, followed by spats of good size driven by an easterly wind. For the first time in many a day he was cheerful, despite the weather, but he carefully avoided analysis of his condition. It might lead to some commitment he really didn't want to make.

The floating bridge connecting Norman's Island to the mainland was a little higher than usual. He stopped at the top of its arch and looked around. Thunderheads were mustering seaward, out where the blue shadow marked the cliffs of Martha's Vineyard. Along the shore of Norman's Island waves were rippling with more than their usual enthusiasm, and a quick scan of the sky showed him that the sea gulls had gone to ground, nestling on the flat roofs of the shopping malls. Warily he pushed the accelerator closer to the floor and put both hands on the wheel to keep from bouncing off the track.

Both houses were still. No smoke trailed skyward, no radios blared, nothing moved until he came to a skidding stop in his own driveway and vaulted out of the car. Sam came around the corner, moving his heavy body on his dainty legs, and trailing a length of rope behind him.

"Great day," he muttered as he knelt beside his pet. The rope was tied loosely around the approximate position where his neck might be. Sam collapsed on the driveway, and continued his meal on the remainder of the rope.

"I should have warned her," Phil told the pig. "Omniverous means that you'll eat anything." He struggled with the knot. "Sisal, huh, old buddy? Your favorite rope. If she had tied you with nylon you'd still be tied." The pig grunted affectionately and rubbed his hairless hide against Phil's leg. The knot came loose, and the pig danced around him in a delightful little jig.

"And how did you and the lady get along today?"

It must have been the wrong question. Sam settled back on four feet and gave him the dismal sort of look that only a pig could muster. "Not so good, Sam?"

His pet shuffled his feet hesitantly. He hated getting wet, and the rain was coming down more heavily. But Sam was no coward. He seemed to shrug himself closer within his thick hide, and started toward the other house at almost a gallop. Due to his curious construction he restricted himself to a brisk trot. But trot he did, and Phil followed along behind him to the other house.

Sam struggled up the small steps to the side door, and banged it open with his rear end. And only then could Phil hear the sound. Somewhere inside, the girl was weeping!

"What's wrong?" Phil brushed by his pet and rushed into the dark kitchen. Charlie was sitting—crouching, perhaps—in her big captain's chair. "Did you hurt yourself?"

So he's finally come, Charlie told herself as she huddled in the chair. It had been too much of a day for her to handle. And here he was, dressed casually for once! She could hear the rain strumming on her roof, but he looked as if not a drop *dared* to fall on him. Curly black hair was as carefully combed as always, with not a gleam of liquid in sight. But his pig, which came over to nuzzle her foot, was dripping all over the floor. Well, I'd rather deal with a wet pig than Mr. Perfect, she told herself grimly.

"Get out of my house," she said weakly. "I've got enough trouble without you breaking in!" She knuckled at her eyes to stop the leakage. No sense in showing *him* my weaknesses, she told herself as she sniffled and reached vainly for a handkerchief.

"Hey, I didn't break in. The door was open." Said softly, with just a touch of concern.

"Then your pig did," she muttered. How *dared* he look so concerned? It was all a come-on, and he wouldn't have caught her in that pig-minding trap this morning if she hadn't been under the influence of the painkillers.

"Your pig did it, and then you followed him. Which makes you an accessory after the fact to breaking and entering!"

"I don't quite remember it that way," he said as he sauntered across the room. "I took two years of pre-law, you know."

"No, I don't know," she snapped back at him as she struggled to her feet. "And I don't want you to tell me about it!"

He said something else to her, in a soft, dulcet voice, but suddenly the words went right over the top of Charlie's head. And he kept talking, mesmerizing her with his voice alone. She still understood not a word. Her mind was squirreling around within its own cage, trying to find some answer to the new and strange feelings that assaulted her. Not anger. For the first time in their relationship anger was not ruling her mind.

He paused, and the silence became heavy on her shoulders. Only the patter of the rain, Sam's heavy breathing, and the tick of her pendulum wall clock punctuated the silence. Any minute now, she told herself, almost in panic, he's going to roar at me—or say something nasty.

Instead he opened his arms to her, and she walked straight into them like a zombie, tears dripping down both cheeks. What are you *doing*, you little fool? she asked herself, but there was no answer. Instead she put her arms around his waist, and his own arms closed behind her like a gate shutting in a safe and secure world from the turbulence outside. She turned her head to one side and nestled up against his shirt, and warmth filled her.

Her sobs died out, and the tears stopped running. She sniffled again; he pushed her away slightly, and offered her a clean handkerchief. "I always carry a spare," he said as he dabbed at her eyes.

"Do you really?" It was an insignificant fact, but her mind snatched at it and marveled.

"Yeah, really. Blow your nose."

She did. "You sound like my house mother," she told him as she returned the handkerchief. There was another moment of silence. He pulled her close against him again. She could feel the strong steady pounding of his heart and smell the sweet sharpness of his after-shave lotion.

"Tell me about your day," he coaxed.

It was almost as if he had pulled the plug on the storage tank of her memories. The words ran out in a confused mixture as one of his hands patted her back comfortably.

"I couldn't even dress myself," she began. "Most of my clothes are pullovers, and without my right hand I couldn't button a button or fasten a snap or pull a zip—well, I couldn't. So I ended up with this housecoat." My *ancient* housecoat, she reminded herself. Sister Mary gave it to me, and she's been dead for over ten years!

"And that's why you're barefoot?"

"I—I couldn't find a pair of shoes. One of them is lost, and the door on my closet is jammed and I couldn't bang on it with one hand, and, oh..." she wailed.

"And your hand hurts?"

"Yes."

"What else?"

"I wanted a couple of eggs for breakfast, but my hand slipped and they fell on the floor, and I ended up with two pieces of toast and I couldn't make the gas burner work right—you can't imagine how hard it is to have your right hand—— Well, it is."

He made soothing noises, and gently massaged her shoulder blades. "I would have scraped the eggs up from the floor, washed them off, and eaten the darn things," he said, chuckling.

"So would I, but Sam got to them first."

"I might have known. What else?"

"And then I thought to put Sam out, so I found this old rope and tied it around his neck and set him outside, only he—"

"Only he ate the rope. I know."

"And he ran off, so I thought by the time you came home you'd be rip-roaring mad at me, and I was scared—"

"You were scared about what *I* would say?" Incredible, his frown seemed to say.

"Scared to death. And then I heard the storm coming up, and—I don't like storms. I really don't."

"But all that isn't the worst of it, is it?"

Charlie squirmed around and stiffened to look up at that solemn lined face above her. Can this be? My neighbor, Attila the Hun, being sensitive to my needs? How could he have changed so much? Or is he just setting me up for some heavy come-down?

"No, tell me the rest," he coaxed.

"It's difficult to explain." Nervously she ran her usable hand through her curls. They fell back into exactly the same position. Another sniffle to clear her nose. Tell him the rest? Why don't I just open my mind up and let him rummage around in there in his bare feet?

"Try me." That soothing sound again, two soft words that encouraged all sorts of truths to be exchanged.

"I've been studying and playing the violin since I was eight years old," she said as she ducked her head into his vest again. "It's been my salvation for a long time. Whenever I get wound up too tight I play something, and the music—or the exercise, maybe—relaxes me. Music has been my whole world. And now—"

"And now you can't play," he said, not as a question but as a statement.

"No, now I can't play. My right hand is my bow hand. There's no way that I can hold a bow steadily, or apply the right pressures. Finished. Done. No music for at least six weeks, and maybe longer." She stopped again and looked up at him, towering over her, not realizing that her eyes were giving her away. *And I can't live for six weeks without my music,* they were finishing.

"How bad is your hand?" Somehow or another *his* hand was running through her hair in a gentle soothing movement. Or, she asked herself in a moment of panic, in a sign of possession? Nothing she feared worse than that some hunting stud would move in on her while she was unaware, and try to dominate her whole life. It had happened to her before! She did her best to sound unconcerned.

"My index finger is bruised and my little finger is broken. The others are bruised. And I can't even find the painkillers. I'm going mad."

"Maybe..." He hesitated for the first time. There was so much he didn't know about this woman. "Maybe you should go home to your mother."

"I can't very well," she said, and a deep sigh followed. "Both my mother and father are dead, and I have no siblings. I was raised in the orphanage of the Sisters of Mercy."

"In that case, you have to turn to your neighbors for help."

"I don't have—" His little chuckle interrupted her. She pushed herself away from him and glared up at him suspiciously. "You're the only neighbor I have," she said in a half whisper.

"You'd better believe it. And I'm going to take care of you."

"I'm not sure I'd care for that," she said as she drew away from him.

"Believe me, you'll love it."

"I don't think I could trust you."

That brought a big grin to his face. "Can't trust me? When you know that Sam will be with us every minute? What better chaperon could you have. How silly can you be?"

"That Big City talk is what gets a lot of country girls in trouble," she said morosely, and drew back another few inches to the point where his fingertips rested at her narrow waist. She took a deep breath; escaping his touch was the first step toward freedom. Unfortunately, just at that moment the storm broke over their heads. Lightning slashed at the island, and since the two houses were the only heights in the area, it smashed against their lightning rods and shook the whole house. Charlie froze in position. Within seconds the loud dramatic roll of thunder broke through her paralysis and she jumped forward into the shelter of his arms again.

"There, now," he said quietly as his arms closed around her again. "Men do have more than one use, Charlie."

She shivered for a moment, then regained her control and pushed herself away from him. His fingertips held her for just a fraction of a second more, as if he hated to turn her loose, and then let her go. He's a man who needs putting down, she told herself. Relax for a minute and he'll have you flat on your back. Look after me? Hah! I'd do better by hiring two wolves to look after the sheep. But then, maybe I could distract him a little?

She took another two steps backward, far enough to reestablish her own personal space. She knew damn nothing about distracting the hunting male, but she was going to make an attempt. "I'm hungry," she announced.

"Then we'll feed you," he said, so very amiably that she almost felt ashamed of herself.

"You can cook?"

"Can Campbell sell soup? What would you like?"

"Not soup," she protested. "How about—ham and eggs?"

"Nothing simpler," he replied, and then moved very much closer and whispered in her ear. "You can have the ham, but Sam is very sensitive about this sort of thing, so I generally call it roast beef." His lips actually touched the lobe of her ear, and she shivered.

"As I said," she agreed, fighting off the strange feelings that assaulted her, "beef and eggs. And fresh coffee. That cold stuff I've been drinking all day tastes like dishwater."

He certainly *acted* like a man who knew cooking. Charlie sat back in her captain's chair and tucked her feet up beneath her, and watched with some amazement as he bustled around her kitchen. Sam, who seemed blasé about the whole affair, came around her chair, circled himself a couple of times, and settled into a black lump at her feet.

He whistled while he worked. Something from the *Pirates of Penzance*, perhaps. Charlie, who knew the work note for note, was only guessing. If it *was* a tune from that comic opera, he was missing a whole slew of notes. But beggars couldn't be choosers, as well she knew. And when he stopped in the middle of his work, dashed into her bedroom, and came out with her ankle-high blue down slippers in his hand, she was more than grateful. The floor *was* cold.

"Move over, Sam," he commanded as he knelt in front of her. His pet pig grunted at him, waved his tail derisively, and refused to budge. "Give over, you superannuated damn—" Again the pig scorned him.

"You'd better move, Sam," she said, and immediately the little porker grumbled to his feet and walked around to the side of the chair.

"*My* pet," Phil commented. "I think I'll sue for alienation of affection."

Charlie had a ready retort, but it didn't quite come out. While Sam was moving Phil had pried one of her feet out from under her, kissed the toes gently as if honoring a queen, and slid her slipper on. It was hard to tell whether the kiss or the slipper warmed her, but warm she was. Instead of waiting for the second assault, she put her other foot down, snatched the remaining slipper from his control, and inserted her foot.

"Foul play," he muttered as he hunkered back on his heels and looked up at her. "Not sportsmanlike."

"I haven't washed my feet, and I've been walking around the house all day." It was true, of course, but she thought of it as a lie. After all, she cleaned her floor daily, and if necessary she could walk around barefoot for hours without getting dirty feet.

"It sounds so reasonable that I'm almost willing to accept the excuse," he replied. "For the moment, that is. Now then, Miss MacEnnaly, try your teeth on this fine breakfast."

Strong men take to drink, she told herself fiercely, so I'll take to food! She picked up her fork and went at it, keeping her eyes down on the plate so she wouldn't be caught up in that hypnotic stare. But he was not about to let her off the hook.

"MacEnnaly," he mused. "What sort of a name is that?"

"Scottish," she mumbled as she reached for another piece of toast. "My grandfather came over from the Old Country. He was a great—" What she was about to say choked her. She swallowed hard and looked up to find him grinning down at her. But if Charlie MacEnnaly had one trait going for her it was honesty to a fault.

"He was a what?"

"He was a great fiddler," she said firmly. "He knew all the old ballads and dances and could play up a storm."

"But you're not a fiddler? I don't seem to know the difference."

"I'm a violinist," she said softly. "Grandpa couldn't read a note of music, but he could play so— well—ever so much better than I." She offered him a tasty glare, the sort that said "Bad luck to you and all in your house!" He kept on grinning. Look at that ignorance, she told herself. He doesn't even know he's been cursed!

"Finished with breakfast?" He was already removing her plate.

"Hey, wait," she objected. "There's still a bit of— beef there."

He held the plate almost under her nose until she had devoured the last morsel as she watched the tiny smile play at one corner of his mouth. When he extended the smile a little dimple appeared on his left cheek. She hadn't noticed that before and wondered why.

"Now then, let's get you dressed, Charlie Mac-Ennaly. We're going to move over to my house."

"We what?"

"I wish you wouldn't act so surprised. I've said that I'm going to take care of you. But I can't do a good job when we're in two separate houses. Close your mouth. It isn't nice for a girl your age to stand around with your mouth open."

"Why do I get the impression that this is one great big con game?"

"I don't know. Because you have a suspicious nature?"

"Oh, of course, it's all *my* fault. You know darn well I have good reason to be suspicious of you!" But tears and the long day and the pain had worn her down to a nub, unable to continue the fight at the level it deserved.

"It's just a mental quirk," he assured her as he bustled into her bedroom and rummaged among her clothes. "This is a nice dress."

"It isn't a dress, it's a caftan. And, if you think I'm going to let you put that on me, you've another think coming, Philip Atmor."

"Can't be seen in an old housecoat," he murmured as he laid the rest of his selections out on the kitchen table. "Stockings? No, I guess you could do without. My house is nice and warm. But I can't seem to find a suitable bra."

"Don't you dare," she muttered, sidling out of the chair and backing over to the stove. "Don't you darn dare!"

"And why are we so sensitive?"

Because *we* know that all our bras have front closures, she thought, and I don't intend to let your hands get that close to me. And you know that, too, Mr. Atmor. She brushed her left hand nervously through her russet hair, making it a worse mess than it had been.

"So," he muttered, his face as solemn as sin, "no bra. Well, perhaps it's not necessary. Briefs? Very utilitarian, I must say. I thought you might have something more—erotic. Don't violinists ever have any fun?''

"Leave me alone," she yelled at him. She managed to squeeze by him, pick up the selection of clothing, and dash for her bedroom. Only when the door slammed behind her did she start breathing again.

"It took you long enough," he said as she came out of the bedroom. She had managed everything except for the zip on the caftan. It had stuck at the halfway point, and no amount of prodding or teasing would bring it up.

"I seem to be stuck," she said.

He couldn't help but notice how much like a little girl she sounded, as if she was in a state of shock. But still delightful. All I have to do now, he told himself, is make sure only one of us loses her temper at a time. Or his temper, as the case might be. Lord, what a beauty she is. A summer rose, no less. With all the thorns still on! What was it that Claudia had recommended? If I want to punish her severely all I have to do is marry her! But that, of course, is going just the slightest bit too far. Look what a harridan marriage made of my mother. What I need to do is to get to the "almost married" part. Delicious! Now then, zips.

It was difficult for him to do all the gallantries standing up, so he dropped to one knee, cleared the zip, and gently closed it all the way. His pet pig, intrigued by the situation, came over and gently licked his nose.

"That's enough, Sam."

"Don't be cruel to him," she said. "He's been your friend for—how many years?"

"Thirteen."

"And he's just trying to show how much he loves you."

"Ah. That's what it is. I've been wondering. Let me see, now. I have your medication in my pocket, I changed the announcement on your answering machine, and it's stopped raining. So now I guess all we have to do is head for the other house."

"I still can't find the right shoes," she admitted gloomily. "I can't get across all that wet grass in my slippers."

"Of course you can," he said. "Transportation has been provided." He swept her up in his arms before she could make a statement, and held her there for a moment, smiling gently down into her sparkling green eyes. "Not quite as light as I thought." He shifted her weight, until her breast flattened against his chest. "There, that's better. Come on, Sam."

The procession moved toward the door. He had both hands full, and Charlie could not see what magic he used to open the door, and then close it behind them. He paused out on the step. The clouds had fled, leaving behind the very tail end of a beautiful red and gold sunset.

"Tired already? You could put me down, you know. I'm sure I could make my way—or, better still, I could stay—"

"O, ye of little faith!" He chuckled as he interrupted her, then studied her face. Not perfect by any means, that face. But square and polished and healthy—and at the moment colored with just a little apprehension. She was one of the few girls he knew whose nose fitted the rest of their faces.

"And that's something else I forgot." He pulled her in close to his chest and bent in her direction.

"No, you don't," she said rather weakly. "I didn't go through all this just to provide kisses for a—"

"For a what?"

"I don't remember the name for people who do things like that," she half whispered, hypnotized by his movements. "But don't you dare kiss me!"

"That was the furthest thing from my mind." He grinned down at her. "You said Sam licked my nose to show his affection. And I thought I'd do the same." With which he moved across the three inches that separated their faces and proceeded to lick her nose. She was still sputtering her indignation when they came through the kitchen door of his house, and he set her feet on the floor.

"You've got a nerve," she grumbled. "Nobody has *ever* done that to me before."

"It was just an urge," he admitted. "Just a wild impulse. Little babies are good at nose licking. Maybe we should try for one."

"You—you horrible man." Her hand was aching again, and her anger was working up a head of steam. "Take me back to my own house! At once, do you hear?"

"I hear all right," he answered mournfully. "The spirit is willing, but the flesh is weak. I don't think I could carry you out to the porch. But I wouldn't think of keeping you against your will. Let me hold the door for you."

As determined as he, Charlie started for the open door, but ten steps were all she could handle. She turned around out on his step, and Phil could see the tears forming in those lovely green eyes. He moved to her side and swept her up in his arms again.

"Tomorrow," he promised, pressing her warmth close up against him, "we'll get some rest and get you your painkillers, and if you still want to leave I'll take you back in the morning. Scout's honor. Bargain?"

She nestled in close against his chest. "My hand aches," she sighed.

It was a long restless night. Her two pills the previous night had knocked her out. She didn't want that again. It bothered her, knowing that she would not be in control of her mind and body for even a single second, and so she had compromised with only one pill.

But what with a strange bed, a situation completely beyond the narrow range of her experience, and the ache in her hand, she had slept only in snatches. Once a noise woke her up, and she could see a dark shadow moving quietly across her room. She shifted on the bed restlessly, but the pill overtook her, and she dropped off to sleep again, sprawled out under the covers. Phil Atmor was that dark shadow, frozen in position, having kicked over the wastebasket, praying that she might not wake up. When she became still he went over to the bureau, where he had unpacked her things, and then came ghosting around to the side of the bed.

"Now don't wake up, and don't scream," he muttered, evidently talking to himself. And then, with all the élan of a man who had done the service many a time before on all types and sizes of models, he undressed her, slid her plain cotton nightgown over her head, readjusted the covers, and kissed her gently on her forehead.

On the second occasion, not far from dawn, she woke again, only to find him sitting in the chair by the bed, holding her hand. When she made a feeble protest he kissed her palm, then folded the arm under the sheets, but remained by her side. This time the comfort lulled her into a deep sleep, and when she awoke to the sunshine he was gone. But Sam had lain himself down on the rug beside her and was doing sentry-dog service.

Evidently Phil Atmor had made more than one trip across to her house. The closet door was open, and most of her clothes were on display. I'll be up and about my business, she told herself as she threw back the blanket and swung her feet out on the floor. Sam stretched and slowly hauled himself up on all four feet to move out of the way.

"So I'll get dressed," she told the pig, which grunted in disbelief. "Well, I'll do better today than I did yesterday." She took a step or two toward the windows and the sunshine. She was functioning much better. She stretched and dipped a time or two. Her nightgown reached down to her ankles and surrounded her with warmth.

"My nightgown! I wasn't wearing a nightgown when I came into this house, and he's the only other person who could have—" Sam, who knew a storm signal when he heard it, scrambled underneath the bed. "I'll murder that man," she muttered. "You hear me? Murder that man!" And it wouldn't be too long in the doing, either. She could hear steps outside in the hall. Her eyes searched the room. In the far corner there was a golf club. An old mashie that had long since seen its day. Charlie hobbled in that direction, and managed to pick up the club just as the bedroom door opened behind her.

"Now, you dirty rat," Charlie roared as she turned around, club held high. "I'm going to—" And the words piled up on her lips and came to a screeching halt. An elderly white-haired woman about her own height but four times her weight stood there, a twinkle in her faded blue eyes.

"So you must be Mrs. Atmor?" The woman had a delightful contralto voice.

"I—well," Charlie managed to say. "I'm . . ." Her mind brushed the cobwebs away. What did Phil tell this woman? Charlie asked herself. It could have been anything at all! And I'm sure he's a believer in telling as big a whopper as possible! Watch your tongue, girl!

"I'm—Charlie." It was the best compromise she could arrive at. "And you?"

"And I'm Mrs. Southerland," the old lady said. "You can call me Beth. Now, your Mr. Atmor hired me yesterday afternoon to come in for a time to be his housekeeper. Because of your hand, you know. Obviously you couldn't do any cooking or cleaning or anything. And look at that cast. It certainly looks like a mess."

"It—feels a little better today. And there are lots of things I can't do," she explained. Including kill that man. Maybe I could hire it done! She walked over to the windows and looked out at sky and sea. "How long do you think you'll be with—us?"

"Six weeks, I understand, my dear. Shall we get you dressed? At least that's one of the things that Mr. Atmor mentioned. Now, let's see. What do you think you'd like to wear today?"

"Nothing fancy. One of those A-line shifts, perhaps? Did you see my—Mr. Atmor this morning?"

"Just for a second. He was in a rush. Hold up your arms now while I slide this slip over your head." The woman was humming an old 1950s tune as she settled a dress over the slip. "He didn't tell me what a pretty girl you were, Mrs. Atmor."

He didn't tell me, either, Charlie told herself. Although I don't know why I'd want to hear such a thing! "Thank you, Beth. I'd feel better, though, if you would call me Charlie. Did Philip say when he would be back?"

"No, but he said he would call you. Now, slippers? And then we'll go down for breakfast—good Lord, what is that?"

"That?" Charlie did her best to sound blasé as she looked behind her to see Sam rising to his feet. It wasn't easy. She had barely accustomed herself to the whole idea of pet pigs. "Oh. You mean Sam? That's Philip's mascot. Isn't he beautiful?"

"I may *never* become comfortable with the younger generation," Beth Southerland muttered as she led the way downstairs. "A pet pig?"

Who undressed me last night? Charlie asked herself grimly as she followed the housekeeper down the stairs. Who told somebody that we were married? I'll kill that man!

Sam, who wasn't much of a conversationalist, struggled along behind them, moving sideways because his short legs and large stomach made stair climbing a major project.

CHAPTER FOUR

PHIL ATMOR came home about four o'clock in the afternoon the next day feeling just a little anxious. His life so far, with Charlie in his own home, had been like riding a fast roller coaster. The night before things had been a little more than hectic. If Charlie had wanted to blow her stack she would have telephoned the office, or called the police. Instead, when he'd bounced over the floating bridge he'd been able to see both houses sitting peacefully on top of the hill, and not a patrol car in sight. And so he'd swept up into his driveway and got out of the Porsche, whistling. All of which had confirmed Charlie's earlier estimate.

"He couldn't carry a tune in a bucket," she told Beth Southerland. "Do you suppose he's tone deaf?"

"I haven't any idea," the housekeeper replied. "I've only known him for a few days at most. Is that important? You should know him better than I, my dear!"

"I should." Charlie dropped the edge of the curtain and turned away from the living room window. "But then we women never really know as much about our men as we think, do we?"

"No, I guess perhaps we don't. But for a young bride to say that? I'm astounded." And there, Charlie thought, is my chance to at least restore things by a partial truth.

"Well, to be exact, Beth, Phil and I are not *quite* married yet. We're only engaged."

"I see," the housekeeper said. "I've wondered. What Mr. Atmor wanted is a chaperon? Perhaps he didn't have the time to explain properly, what with your accident being so sudden, and all."

"Yes, that's entirely true," Charlie replied. Mrs. Southerland was too nice a lady to recognize the sarcasm. On that note Phil walked into the house.

"And how are we all?" he called as the side door slammed behind him. Sam, who had been sleeping in the living room, came alive and bolted for him. Beth Southerland faded away into the kitchen with a knowing smile on her face, while Charlie walked casually out into the hall. Her delightful figure and motion looked calm—from the rear. Only a fool could face her without knowing that she was furious.

"Mr. Atmor," she started out. He was kneeling, scratching Sam's neck. He came to both feet and, before she could get in another word, he swooped down on her. Like an octopus, she thought, in the small moment of time she had left to think. "Don't—"

His arms gathered her into his chest, his head came down so that his lips could seal hers, and suddenly the world had become a multicolored rocket ride. Red and yellow and blue fantasies struck at her nervous system, followed by an attack of the shakes as her courage wilted. There was a strange roiling in her stomach, and a shower of sparklers that blinded her. A full symphonic orchestra was playing the "1812 Overture,'' and when they finished a whole division's worth of cannons were firing wildly. And then everything was still.

"Don't what?" he asked innocently as he turned her loose. Charlie blinked both eyes. He was close, not more than six inches away, studying her as if to record and analyze the effect.

"Don't do that," she muttered as she reestablished control. "Don't you ever do that! I want to know why—"

"We'd better step outside," he said, locking on to her left arm. And then yelling, "We're going out for a little walk, Miss Beth! You call us when supper's ready."

"But I..." Charlie fumbled for words, still trying to subdue her unruly passions.

"Walk," he murmured in her ear, and by that time the door had slammed behind them, and they were out on the lawn, Sam close on their heels.

"We'll need to put in a few flowers," he said casually as he drew her away from the house. "And maybe a few vegetables. I always had a vegetable garden at home."

"Well, good luck to you," she snapped as she gave her arm a quick yank and managed to free herself. Her uninjured hand brushed vaguely through her hair and then tugged at the white cotton blouse she was wearing.

"Okay, we're far enough away. What's the beef?"

"You—you unprincipled rogue," she muttered, squaring away in front of him with her hands on her hips. Her face was almost the same color as her hair.

He held up both of his hands between them, palms facing her, for protection.

"I confess. Whatever it was, I confess. Of what am I guilty?"

"You rotten..." She stamped her foot. Sam dodged out of the way.

"I think we can take all that as said." She glared at him, so tense that her entire body quivered.

"Damn you. Who undressed me last night?"

"I confess," he repeated, but with a grin tugging at the corners of his mouth. "I knew you wouldn't be able to sleep with those tight clothes on, and you were so restless that I figured my best bet would be to put you in a nightgown. But it was too dark for me to see anything."

"You're totally amoral, aren't you? Is that all you've got to say about it?"

"Not at all. I wish it could have been lighter. I'm sure it was a delightful view, even though I couldn't see it. Next question?"

"Arghhh!"

"Careful. Don't choke on it!"

Calm down, she told herself. He's just getting at you. Cold, calm, disdainful, that's what. She wrestled with herself, and won. In a steady, cold tone she asked, "And why is it that Mrs. Southerland thinks we're married?"

"Now that's a major problem." He shook his head and produced a massive sigh. "When I first talked to Mrs. Southerland it became apparent that she was the old-fashioned type, who wouldn't look with favor on two unmarried people living alone in the house. I'm sure you know the type. And my secretary, who happens to be her cousin, was kind enough to tell me that Beth is one of the world's biggest gossips."

"So you told her we were married? Just to escape embarrassment?"

"Not exactly, Charlie. It was a spur-of-the-moment thing, but I did it to save your reputation. You're famous, my dear. I wouldn't want any scandal to—"

"All right," she sighed. "All right. You don't have to pour it down with a ladle. You did it all for my benefit. I believe you. Of course, there's a world full of folk who wouldn't, but that's not important."

"Exactly. Boy Scout oath. I wish you sounded more as if you believed it."

"Don't push your luck. I've just told Beth that there's a misunderstanding. That we're not married, merely engaged."

"And she didn't quit? Or say something nasty?"

"Not a word. She just smiled as if she'd known it all along. Now, how long do we have to go on with this charade?"

"Not long. Certainly not more than three or four weeks. Not until you can handle things for yourself."

"Let it come soon," she prayed. "But remember: this isn't a trial marriage, and I'm not interested in any fly-by-night affairs. You can have the name, but not the game. Lay a finger on me, Mr. Atmor, and I'll serve you up your most valued possessions in a stew!"

"I wouldn't dream of imposing," he lied. "But to make this little act play in Peoria there'll have to be a certain amount of 'my darling' and some passionate osculation a few times a day. For the audience, of course.''

"Semi-passionate," she stated firmly. "The way old married couples do. I'm not playing young love and the honeymoon scene!''

It was a better compromise than Phil had hoped to achieve. So he kissed her—semi-passionately—and just at that moment Mrs. Southerland rang the dinner bell. To test his luck he put an arm around her. She stiffened, but there was no violent reaction. He pulled her a little closer, and the pair of them walked sedately back to the house.

"It's good to see young love in the springtime of life." Beth Southerland grinned from ear to ear as they sat down at table, and she began serving the dinner. "How long have you two been engaged?"

"It hardly seems any time at all," Phil reported.

"It seems like forever," Charlie said at exactly the same time. A horn sounded from outside.

"That'll be my granddaughter come to drive me home," Beth said. "Now you'll remember, Charlie, to leave all the cleanup for me. I'll be in early in the morning and get it all put away. By the way, what would you want for dinner tomorrow?"

"Ham," Charlie said quickly. Phil leaned over and kissed her very romantically, accompanying the act with a pinch to her bottom. Charlie yelped.

"We never have ham," he told the housekeeper, speaking loudly enough to cover the mutterer sitting next to him. "Fish, perhaps. Haddock?"

Charlie, surreptitiously rubbing her bottom where the pinch still smarted, decided not to let him off that easily. "We never have ham. My—er—fiancé has an allergy problem." She settled back in her chair with a self-satisfied grin on her face.

"Oh, I didn't know," Beth commented as she fluttered around, picking up her knitting bag and her wide-brimmed hat.

"And not just ham," Phil told her with that solemn look on his face. "I'm also allergic to certain types of animals and people who make too much noise for their own good." The old housekeeper gave them a strange look, clapped on her hat, and swept out of the door.

"You shouldn't tell so many lies," she admonished primly.

"You should eat your dinner before it gets cold," he returned. The rest of the meal was eaten in cold, cold silence.

Three weeks later, after having lived in an armed camp all the while, Charlie went off to her doctor's office, where the original cast was removed, and a much smaller one substituted, one that left her thumb free, and gave a little more flexibility to the fingers which had only been bruised.

"It feels as if you've taken ten **pou**nds off my hand," she told the doctor.

"It looks fine, Miss MacEnnaly. Everything's healing as it should. Just continue being careful. I'll give you a prescription for codeine tablets to go with the new cast. You won't need the strong ones any further. I'll put you down for another visit a week from today."

His nurse rushed her out of the door to make room for the next patient before she had a chance to ask a question. Which was just as well, Charlie thought. The only question she'd really meant to ask was ''How do you get a glass of poisonous hemlock in these parts?'' Philip Atmor was most definitely getting under her skin!

She drove slowly back to the island, keeping one eye on her watch. Sam was on the back seat of her car, fast asleep, as usual. Any dog in the world would have whined and barked and grumbled at being left alone in her Jeep; Sam never even thought about jumping out of the open windows. This was Beth Southerland's half day off. Charlie wanted to take advantage of being alone to walk the beach and think about her problems.

She parked the car beyond the houses and patted Sam on his square little snout. The pig came awake in a rush, and followed her awkwardly out onto the sand. Charlie took a deep breath. The wind was out of the southeast, promising warmer weather. She slipped out of her shoes, managed with one hand to untie the ribbon that held her brilliant hair in a ponytail, and started off slowly, going down to the beach.

There was a glory to the feel of the soft brilliantly white sand. She edged closer to the tidal mark, and let the waves cool her toes. Life seemed infinitely better.

''Heel, Sam,'' she commanded, and the little porker moved behind her right heel and began to follow, his head held high, his little feet prancing like a show horse's. Except for the absence of my music, she thought, things are—tolerable. In fact, there was a great deal of enjoyment in her nightly duels with the pompous Mr. Atmor. And he—he was a great deal of man! Sam must have seen her blush. He grunted a couple of times and moved closer.

"Heel," she commanded, but Sam pulled away and dashed out into the surf to cool off. Pigs, whose internal structure made the animal the best source of tests and vaccines for mankind, had one serious lack. It possessed no sweat glands for ventilation. Which was the reason why pigs, when there was no other water supply handy, would wallow in mud holes. Although Sam would have preferred clean pure water for his duckings, and rated salt water very low, when nothing else was available he sought out the sea. And was an excellent swimmer. Now he splashed and squealed for attention.

"I'm daydreaming," Charlie yelled to him. "Don't bother me." Not since her tenth birthday had she done ballet. Now, on this cool, comfortable sand, she felt the urge. A pirouette or two, a spin, letting her skirts swing wide and high around her thighs, a vaulting jump and an awkward landing, which pitched her three or four feet out into the ocean, trying frantically to keep her right hand and its cast out of the water!

She came back to shore on her knees, one hand above her head, like a cavalry flag. Sam's flat nose butted her in the right direction as the waves washed her clean. She came back laughing as she had not laughed in so many years that she could not remember. At least, not since she had moved into the hands of Maestro Oistraka, the stern taskmaster who had

driven all the pleasures out of her curriculum and replaced them with violin solos. Sam was standing at the
very edge of the tide, looking straight at her and
shaking his head dolefully. He loved to bathe, did her
little pig, but humans hardly seemed to know how to
go about it. Charlie looked down at her hand. The cast
was dry. She gave a big sigh. Her doctor had spent an
hour during her last checkup lecturing about dry casts!

"There's hope for the human race," Charlie announced grandly. The pig backed up the beach a little
way, as if he doubted the statement very much. Still
laughing, Charlie came up out of the water, shook
herself like some shaggy dog, and ran her long hair
through a single-handed wringer.

Down the beach, about a hundred yards away, she
could see an old wooden pier. "Come on, Sam," she
called as she started to trot down toward this interesting new development.

It was about as rickety a wharf as New England
possessed, wobbling out toward the other shore a good
twenty feet, but swaying with each assault of the
waves. Moored at its far end was a flat-bottomed
rowing boat, as rickety as the pier itself. Charlie
moved cautiously out on the pier and stared down at
the boat, a good six feet below her. The wooden ladder that reached down to it was too difficult for a one-
handed girl to master.

"Too much," she announced to Sam, who had
come warily out to stand beside her. The pig considered the boat from every angle and then squealed a
warning. "All right," she assured him. "I *see*."

But as she offered the assurance she leaned farther over the edge for a better look, and Sam obviously felt that a demonstration was needed. He grumbled at her, edged between her and the side of the pier, and then lost his balance and landed in the sea beside the boat.

Charlie, knowing how well the pig could swim, cheered him on, and then took a deep breath as Sam came up out of the water with his forequarters and rested his weight on the side of the boat. Almost at once water began to bubble up from the floorboards, and in a moment it was half full. Sam grunted a couple of times, looking up to be sure that Charlie was watching, and then came off the boat and swam in to the shore. The rickety old boat bounced upward and began to drain. The rickety old pier shook as Charlie ran for the shore, and the pair of them, pig and girl, met on the sand.

"Okay, Okay, I get the message," Charlie said. "I suppose there are lots who wouldn't. Come on, Sam, let's go home the wrong way around!"

Her beautiful hair floated in a sort of halo around her head, and she was filled by a feeling of euphoria. "I'm all right, and you're all right and he's all right!" she chanted as they ran. And with not a regret on her mind, having forgotten all the stupid things Phil had said at breakfast, she led her little procession, humming "Yankee Doodle" as they went.

A piece of land as small as Norman's Island didn't take a great deal of running around to come full circle. Charlie blessed the shortness of the path. She was out of breath when they came up behind the house, and had to stop at the coping of the stone wall to catch her breath. Her passage had disturbed the family of finches living in the scrub apple tree. They took to the sky and scolded her. Sam came to a stop beside her, panting. It doesn't seem fair, Charlie told herself. He's obviously overweight, and yet he's barely out of breath.

But Sam was doing something else, too. He was not only a companion, he was also a watch pig. And he was watching something that Charlie could not see. The little porker stood in a pointer stance for several minutes, continually twisting his head to look up at her for directions. And then he grunted and hurtled himself toward the corner of the house. Fat, short-legged, middle-aged—all these he was, but when he lowered his head and began to race forward he was like a bullet out of a gun. Somewhere, in some hidden corner of Sam's genes, was the memory of the charging boars of his wild ancestry. He bared those extremely sharp teeth and squealed in rage.

"Sam!" The call was wasted. He was around the corner and out of sight before she could make herself heard. But not more than two seconds later he had arrived *somewhere*, and there were screams tormenting the wind. Feminine screams.

"Oh, Lord," Charlie murmured as she stepped her way cautiously across the stones of the back yard. A door slammed—the kitchen screen door that gave access to the entry hall, but not to the house. More screams. When Charlie arrived on the scene there was Sam guarding the door, his little snout aimed inward and a belligerent look on his face. Trapped in the little cul-de-sac between the screen door and the locked house door was a pair of women.

"Sam!" No response. "Damn you, Sam!" Those were the magic words. The mini-pig lowered himself gently on to his stomach, still maintaining the menacing watch, while Charlie came up behind him, puffing for breath. The screaming stopped.

"You can come out now," Charlie called. The first woman was tall and thin, some fifty years old or more, dressed in the finest pale blue silk afternoon dress that money could buy. A saucy little sun hat held her blond white hair most carefully in place. But her hands were trembling as she opened the outer screen door. The second was a younger woman, perhaps thirty-something, a suicide blonde—even at this distance Charlie could see that. She too was elegantly over-dressed, but in lace blouse, pencil-thin white pants, and two-inch heels.

"What—what is that thing?" the older woman demanded. She turned sideways to squeeze by Sam. The pig's eyes followed her every movement. It would appear that the younger woman didn't dare the challenge. She stayed in the little entry hall, her hand on the screen door, prepared to slam it shut if anything happened.

"That's Sam," Charlie said, as if that were the only explanation needed.

"I didn't ask who, I asked what," the older woman snapped haughtily. She had her head thrown back like an aristocrat about to dispense bread to the peasant crowds. Her voice was slightly cracked but still held the timbre of command.

Sam rolled over on his back, looking for accolades. I've done my part, his look said. Well?

"Good job." Charlie fell to one knee and scratched his broad belly, where compliments should rightly be paid. One could almost hear the pig purr. "This is Sam," she told the elder woman. "Sam's a mini-pig. A pet pig. Sam and I live here. Now, just who are you?"

"My *son* lives here," the matriarch said in a very chilly tone. The younger woman gasped.

"Well yes, him too," Charlie admitted, blushing. "He ought to be along any minute." He'd *better* be along any minute now, she told herself. This is too much for a growing girl to handle. His *mother* has come among us? The explanations ought to be magnificent, and *I'm* not making them. "And here he comes now."

And here he *did* come; the Porsche zoomed into the drive with its customary zeal, hesitated for a moment, and then crawled up the rest of the way. Trying his best to think up a story to meet the circumstances, Charlie thought, and couldn't suppress the giggle.

Phil Atmor bounced out of the car like some jovial but skinny Santa Claus. Charlie took a step or two in his direction and then stopped to let Sam do his welcoming bit. Phil was crouching, petting the pig, when Charlie came within reach, and he reached for her with his unoccupied hand. "Hello, darling," he announced briskly. "It's been one hell of a day." And then he pulled her head closer and whispered in her ear, "What the hell is going on?"

"How should I know? They arrived out of the clear blue sky. The white-haired one claims to be your mother. The other one doesn't seem to have a tongue. But your mother seems to want an explanation about you and I and Sam all living in the same house. And I don't have one to give. That's your line of work, not mine."

"Boy," he grumbled as he gave Sam one last chuck behind his ears. "You're a great help, you are."

"Always," she muttered as he crushed her to his side and began walking her back to the house. "I'm with you forever. I'll cheer you on even in front of your mother, *my love*. She *is* your mother, isn't she?"

"Just take your cues from me," he muttered, and then looked up as if seeing the other pair for the first time. He stopped, and a broad smile spread across his face. Doing her part, Charlie kept her eyes on him, smiling as best she could, like a lovesick calf. It had been a long time since she had been smitten by a male. Henry Lowell, wasn't it? When I was nine years old?

"Mother!" He dropped his grip around Charlie's waist and went toward his mother, both hands extended. "Mother!" And isn't that a fine piece of dialogue? Charlie thought. Even the worst of rock music contained more than two words, or was it three? Mother and son were embracing enthusiastically. And I wish they'd cut that out, Charlie thought angrily, and stopped in her tracks. Can I be jealous of Phil hugging his own mother? Good Lord! What am I coming to?

The Atmors, mother and son, broke their embrace. His mother took him by the hand and tugged him toward the younger woman. "And you remember, Philip, little Emily Atwater?"

"Little Emily Atwater?" Either he was a consummate actor, or he just didn't remember. Not until little Emily qualified her position in life.

"Emily Freitas," she explained. "I've resumed my maiden name since the funeral."

"Well, Emily Freitas," Phil said. He extended both hands, but the girl was more enthusiastic than that. She walked into his arms, threw herself around his neck, and held on for dear life. For a moment Phil stood there like a statue, and then gradually his arms slipped around the blonde's waist and hugged her closely.

"Look at that," Charlie muttered. Sam nosed at her bare toes, reminding her that her shoes were still in the car. "All right, all right," she said, and headed for her car.

"Don't run off, Charlie," Phil called after her.

"I won't. I have to get my shoes." Well, that's better than telling him I'll choke to death standing here watching this—this Emily making a fool of herself. Or of me? Maybe I should just go back and yell, "Get your flaming hands off my man!" But of course that wouldn't do. Phil has never said anything about *him* and *me* being *us*. And I haven't been too easy on him the last several days. Why am I crying?

It took her much longer than expected to find her shoes on the back seat of her car, and more time than that to put them on her feet. But by that time her eyes were dry, and if anyone asked about the color in her cheeks she could always claim that she was wind-blown. "C'mon, Sam," she said, "let's go face the music."

They were all in the kitchen, sitting at the heavy circular table, when she and Sam came in. "Ah, there you are," he said as he stood up, a big jovial look on his face. Explanation time, Charlie thought, and I'll bet this one is going to be a dandy.

"I'd forgotten that Beth has Wednesday afternoons off. I was just telling my mother what a gem of a housekeeper she is."

And I've got nothing to say to that, Charlie thought, and so she stood there and looked at him expectantly. He grimaced at her, knowing that his back was to the two visitors.

"I hope we can find something for dinner tonight."

Cooperative old Charlie, she told herself grimly. "I hope so too."

He fumbled for another idea or two. "Oh, Mother." He turned around as if struck by a sudden thought. "You haven't met Charlie, have you?"

"Yes," his mother replied. Chill winds for June! "When her—pig scared us half to death, if you'll remember. Just who—?"

"Well, actually, it's *my* pig," he interrupted. And then added a little dig. "Sam and I have been together, for, oh, thirteen years. Ever since both you and Emily went out of my life! Both in the same year, to be exact."

Emily looked as if she was about to cry. "We have to talk, Phil. Later on, when we can be alone?" There was desperation in the girl's voice, a sort of pleading.

He shrugged his shoulders and turned his attention back to his mother. "Charlie is a world-famous musician, Mother. Well, her name is Charlotte MacEnnaly. She's played as a soloist in London and Berlin and Paris, and at the Bavarian festival—"

"And in Vienna," his mother interrupted. "I heard her play at the *Stattsoper*. Christmas, two years ago, I believe. With the Vienna Boys' Choir, and the Deutchessymphonique. Isn't that right?"

"That's right," Charlie agreed. "Or was it three years ago? It's hard to remember."

"I'm sure it must be," Mrs. Atmor added.

And all of a sudden I'm a member of the "in" crowd, Charlie thought. The glacier has become a warm Mediterranean shore or something. But she hadn't another thing to add. Silence weighed on the room.

"Beth left us cold cuts and a casserole," Charlie offered. Phil gave her a look of gratitude.

"You've injured your hand," Mrs. Atmor commented, as if seeing the cast for the first time. "Something broken?"

"A finger on my bow hand," Charlie admitted. "It makes it impossible to play, and difficult to get things done. But Phil's taking care of me, and at least I can warm a casserole."

This was another sentence hanging in the air. Nobody offered to help with the casserole. Nobody even brought the subject up. In fact, just the opposite. "I must have a shower," Emily interjected. "There's so much—dust in this corner of the world. I couldn't bear to do another thing without a wash. Phil, would you bring in our things, and show me to a room?"

"The very thing," his mother added. "I could use a lie down and a shower myself."

"We only have one bathroom," Charlie pointed out.

"One bathroom? Why, that's hardly civilized!"

"Now, Emily, you have to take the sweet with the sour. Just the sheer pleasure of seeing Philip makes up for it all."

"Of course it does." Emily, reminded of her lines, looked up at Phil apologetically.

"You can take the two rooms at the head of the stairs," Charlie suggested. The pair of them nodded and headed for the second floor. Phil bent down in the middle of the kitchen and scratched at Sam's ear.

"Damned if Sam isn't losing weight," he mused.

"And he darn well ought to," Charlie said. "I took him to the vet's. He weighed in at seventy-two pounds. The vet says that for a sedentary pig he has to lose twenty pounds, or it's off to the slaughterhouse. I put him on a crash diet. See that you don't meddle with it!"

"Twenty pounds? Dear Lord, you'll kill him."

"Yes, well I'm eager to hear what your next explanation is going to be."

"I haven't said a word but the truth," he protested.

"Since your mother's come," Charlie reminded him. "I know that, and I'm wondering how long you can hold to the straight and narrow. If I were a betting woman I'd bet ten dollars even that you can't last beyond the next forty-eight hours. Bet?''

He gave her a cold look and no answer. She nagged him again. ''I'll bet the temptation is irresistible. Think up something good while you're carrying the suitcases up to their rooms.''

''The suitcases?''

''I'd swear there was an echo in this room. The suitcases. Your mother brought four, and your— friend has three more. Go lift that bale, tote that barr'l.''

''You are a mean, hard-hearted woman, Charlie MacEnnaly.''

''Bite your tongue, Mr. Atmor!''

''I think I'd do better if I bit you, Miss Macelheny,'' he grumbled as he started for the door. Sam followed nose-to-heel.

''MacEnnaly,'' she yelled after him. ''It's a devil of a note when you can't even get a girl's name right!''

He turned around in the half-open door and gave her a big grin. ''But, you see, there are so *many* girls,'' he said mournfully, and then ducked as one of the unbreakable plates came at him like a wild Frisbee looking for the kill!

Although it was a simple dinner, Charlie had quite a time struggling with all the details, and neither of the other women made any effort to help. When Phil came through the kitchen on his way to his study she filed a protest.

''Well, my mother is quite old,'' he replied. ''I don't think we could expect *her* to help.''

"Then how about that other witch?" Charlie said belligerently.

"Emily? I don't think she can spare the time. In fact, that's why I'm going to my study. She evidently has a great many serious problems, and I've agreed to meet her in—" he pulled back his sleeve and consulted his gold wristwatch "—in ten minutes."

"Yes, I can see you have problems," she snapped.

"Hey, no fighting, Charlie. We *did* arrange a truce, as I remember."

"Yes." Charlie lowered her voice but the words came out vituperatively. "Yes indeed. We agreed on a truce. For the purpose, as I remember, of me being able to rest until my hand gets well. Am I remembering it all wrong?"

"No, not at all." That pompous-executive tone again saying "Look, I come among you to spread joy and light in your miserable lives!" Damn the man, she thought. Just as soon as my hand is free of this cast I'm going to—I don't know what I'm going to, but I'm going to!

"Don't shake like that," he ordered. "You'll give the show away if you're afraid."

"I'm not afraid, Mr. Atmor." Said coolly, each word enunciated in capital letters for emphasis. "I'm not afraid. I'm angry. Maybe you'd better make an appointment so we can talk over *my* terrible problems?"

"Yes, yes, of course," he muttered as he hurried away. Charlie watched him run. The running man, she thought. A coward of the first degree. Every time I conclude that he's a big, strong, intellectual man he turns into a meathead!

Sam came over and licked the tip of her shoe. Lovable old Sam. "Sam, I might take you with me when I run away from this den of iniquity." But the pig wanted out. She took him to the door and watched as he headed straight for his own private swimming pool. After carefully checking the water, he splashed in and began to swim his lengths.

"What a good idea," Charlie muttered as she went back to setting the table in the kitchen.

"Eating in the kitchen?" Mrs. Atmor came in dressed for dinner at Antoine's. "I don't think that's the best idea."

"Probably not," Charlie said determinedly, "but it's the closest place to the stove, and that's as far as I can carry the food. Unless you would care to do the work for me?"

An astonished expression came over the woman's face. Her lip trembled for a moment, and then she turned and went back out into the living room. And that drops me back at least ten percentage points in the standing, Charlie told herself as she tried to complete the place settings. I wonder if she ran because she doesn't want to work, or because she doesn't want to interfere, or if she's never set a table before?

It was a very intriguing question. "I've got to look into that a great deal more," she murmured as she tried to arrange the cold cuts in a neat platter.

"I'm sure you must." Phil Atmor, coming in behind her, and standing casually in the center of the floor. "May I help?"

"Yes." Charlie gave a great sigh of relief. "First, don't stand in the middle of the floor. Second, take that hot casserole out of the oven—I can't do it one-handed—and third, go let Sam in, and make sure he shakes himself dry on the porch, not in my kitchen."

"Another misinterpretation." He offered her that lopsided grin that made him look so endearingly homey. "I meant to help you look into that something that's bothering you, not to help with the dinner. That's woman's work."

Charlie whirled around, forgetting the skillet in her left hand. He was still grinning, but he backed off a pace or two. "But I will let Sam in," he promised.

"Did anyone ever tell you," she asked, speaking through clenched teeth, "that you are a thoroughly objectionable man?"

"Only you. My secretary, Claudia Sylvia, thinks I'm a wonderful young fellow."

"Watch my lips," she muttered. "Take the casserole out of the oven and put it in the middle of the table before I cut you up just north of your pant pockets! Got it?"

Again that devilish grin. "Now, I think I've got it! Just stay with me, sweetheart. I'm a very slow learner."

Charlie, who had turned her back on him momentarily, wheeled around to say something expressive about the *sweetheart* business, saw Emily and his mother come into the kitchen, both with their noses in the air, and swallowed her comment. So it hadn't been a very *long* interview with Emily, Charlie told herself. Is that good because he didn't want to listen, or bad because he made a quick decision in *that woman's* favor? Another puzzle? I'll be up all night with the problems I've already got on my plate. There had better not be any more tonight.

"Sit here, Mother." Like a properly dutiful son, Phil held the best chair for his mother, and then seated Emily as well. Charlie shook herself out of her rage and lifted the cover from the casserole. "It's family-style," she announced. "Everyone serve themselves." Sam came over beside Charlie's usual chair. He was an intelligent little pig. In just a few days he had learned that Phil might scatter more crumbs, but what fell from Charlie's plate would probably be tastier.

Charlie started for her own chair; nobody was offering to help, another stab at her conscience. And I'll remember them all, she told herself grimly. All these little wounds. She pulled the chair out.

"Oh, I forgot something!" Phil exclaimed. The two ladies looked up at him as he walked to the refrigerator and whipped out a bottle of Dom Pérignon. "I have an announcement to make, and a toast to pledge, and I'm sure you'll all be pleased and astonished!"

With a skill that bespoke a very great deal of practice with champagne bottles, he popped the cork and poured a libation for each of them. "Now what?" Charlie muttered, *sotto voce.*

"Don't worry," he whispered back as he came around to stand at her side. "I've got it all figured out. You'll all be pleased and astonished."

So, being as curious as any normal female, Charlie hushed. He checked to see that all had full glasses in their hands. "Oops. Forgot." He bent down and poured a little of the bubbly into Sam's dish. "Have to include all the members of the family, right?"

They all stared at him as if he might have lost a marble or two.

"The announcement is simple," he said, and there was a grin on his face a half-mile wide. "I have decided to marry and provide the Atmor empire with a new heir."

"Hear, hear," his mother said as she lifted her glass.

"That's wonderful," Emily said in her shrill voice.

"And so I propose a toast to the beautiful lady who has agreed to marry me." He lifted his glass. "Here's to Charlotte Rose MacEnnaly, my future bride!"

Charlie dropped into her chair, losing a portion of her drink in the doing. She glared up at him, expecting God to strike him dead, but there was no divine intervention. In desperate need of assistance, Charlie drained her glass in one swallow and held it up for a refill.

Phil moved cautiously to her side, and sat down while she finished her second dose. "It's customary for the loving couple to exchange a kiss," he announced as he took her glass from her trembling hand and set it aside.

"You certainly like to live dangerously," she grumbled in his ear as he pulled her close and hugged her.

"I'll explain it all tomorrow," he whispered.

"You should live so long," she muttered. And before she could make another angry remark he kissed her. It was one of his patented "Let's get the little woman more confused than before" kisses, complete with fireworks, warmth and shivers. It was also one of those that a normal girl would have just hated to have end. But it did.

And as she dazedly looked around the table at the other females present Charlie sighed. Well, he certainly is half right, she told herself. He may not have *pleased* anybody here at this table, but he certainly has *astonished* us all!

CHAPTER FIVE

CHARLIE hurried down the stairs early the next morning, dressed in T-shirt and jeans, hoping to get in three or four more left jabs in her running battle with Philip. The discussion the previous night had been far from satisfactory. It hadn't been a good fight, either. He'd bobbed and weaved and evaded until it had seemed his tongue might have tied itself into knots. And at the end of all that he had astounded her again, slipping a lovely blue sapphire ring on her finger.

She might have raged, but she'd been very tired and it was a delightful ring. She had been in bed for almost an hour before questions had arisen, and, since she'd dropped off to sleep at about the same time, the questions had faded into the dream that had followed. A very strange dream, having to do with wild nights and robust men and sex. About which she knew less than nothing.

But the questions were back this morning, and they caused her to stop halfway down the stairs and mutter something unprintable.

"And good morning to you, Charlie." Mrs. Beth Southerland was back, standing there at the foot of the stairs with a big smile on her face.

"Good morning, Beth. Is he still here?"

"No, I'm afraid not. He was driving out just as I came in. Breakfast?"

"Darn. I wanted so much to catch him before he left. Breakfast? I suppose. Coffee and toast, perhaps."

"You need more than that, young lady. You have to build up your strength. Getting married takes a lot out of a girl. It can be a very—physical activity."

"Is that so?" There was no doubt about what Beth was insinuating. Charlie had difficulty stopping the blush that formed. She came down the stairs and followed the housekeeper into the kitchen.

"Was there something you particularly wanted from the mister?"

Think fast, Charlie told herself. Romance is in the air. "Nothing important," she murmured. "It's just— he only kissed me once this morning and I wanted to . . . well."

There was a broad grin on the housekeeper's face. "That's delightful, child. Why don't you go into the city at noon and have lunch with him? Here's your coffee."

"I don't think I'd dare." Charlie looked up and found that big grin again. I won't go because I'm sure I'll blow my stack, Charlie told herself. But obviously Beth thinks there's some other reason. Dream on, lady. One fine day soon I'm going to huff and puff and blow this house down!

Sam heard the noise. He came waddling in from the living room, and nosed at her ankles. He grunted once or twice, and made a halfhearted beeline for the side door.

"I hope that—pig is house-trained," Beth suggested.

"Perfectly. He wants out now."

"Well, I can't make head nor tail of him. He's been running around the house like mad, climbing up on his hind legs to look out the window."

"That's easy enough to decode. He needs his bath."

"The pig needs a bath? Of course." Beth Southerland shook her head and sighed. "What'll they think of next?"

"Don't ask me," Charlie said. "I don't believe what I already know. C'mon, Sam." The ponderous little pig came to heel immediately, and they proceeded out into the yard, where Charlie turned on the lawn sprinkler, and the pig plunged into the spray with a squeal of delight. Charlie watched for a moment, then wandered over to her own house and unlocked the door.

The place smelled musty after being shut up for three weeks. "First things first," she said, and went around opening all the windows. There was a delightful sea breeze blowing, and the sun was June warm. She stepped out onto the minuscule front porch, actually only a square piece of concrete some eight by ten feet, and startled a lone bird into flight. The bird was hardly more startled than Charlie. She jumped back into the shelter of the doorway and watched as the beautiful gray-and-white herring gull swung clumsily a few feet away and landed again.

Something's wrong with his left wing, Charlie thought. Softhearted Charlie. She went back into the kitchen, opened a can of sardines with her electric can opener, and set it out on the porch. From her living room window, being careful not to disturb the curtains, she watched as the bird hobbled back to the porch and devoured the offering.

Now what? she asked herself as she wandered over to the piano. Why is it so darned lonely around here? Her usable hand picked up her violin and her fingers wandered over the frets. The new cast had left enough of her right hand free to at least hold the bow, but she had no control over pressure or emphasis, so she tucked the violin under her arm and tried using it as a sort of mandolin. Thumb and forefinger plucked at the strings as her left hand established the notes. The ancient violin responded with the full range of its mellow voice. Gently, carefully, she plucked out the notes of her favourite *liebeslied*. It was hard work. She tried it once more, then carefully laid the instrument down on the piano top.

"It's a start," she told herself. Not the full range of the bowing, of course, but something. Yes, it *is* a start, she thought. But a start to what? For months we have run a raging feud between us, Phil and I, and I've thought Phil Atmor was my worst enemy. And now, all of a sudden—he's what? Not an enemy, that's for sure. Not a friend, either. Despite his pompous know-it-all self, he's more than a friend. She held her ring up and let its jewel sparkle in the shaft of sun through the window. Why isn't it true? Because, evidently, I'm the only one feeling the effect. Proximity—is that it? I know so little about men that being this close to one has knocked me off my feet? Damn! I've got to do something—anything! She was startled by a squawk from the front door step. The bird? The poor darn gull!

She was out of the side door before the thought had even gelled. Sam, still enjoying the lawn sprinkler, gave it all up and dashed across the yard to her. He shook himself, like some big shaggy dog, and sprayed Charlie and her neighborhood. "Hey, cut that out," she muttered, but she was smiling as she did so. Sam grunted a little appreciation, and then followed behind her as she walked slowly around the corner of the house. The herring gull was still sitting on the front porch, his right wing swept up into his body, the left dragging, outstretched, broken or damaged.

"Sam," she commanded. "Stand. Guard." The pig came to a pointer position and froze. Charlie turned slowly and walked back around the house. Out of the bird's sight, she ran. In the kitchen she had a stored cat's cage, an open wire container used for shipping small animals on aircraft. Cage in hand, she ran back out and around the house. Sam was still in his guard position. The gull watched warily, his head moving from side to side, his long sharp beak held up as a weapon. And that, Charlie knew, was a major problem. Wild birds didn't care to be handled. A beak as sharp as the gull's could do major damage. But she had to try.

Still moving gently, Charlie moved up onto the step, singing softly. The bird shifted his attention from Sam to Charlie, and then back again. She put the cage down and opened the hinged wire top. The gull's attention came back to her, but the beautiful white head was drooping; his yellow beak dropped down onto the concrete, and the little yellow spot on its lower mandible showed in the sun.

Charlie moved closer; the bird stirred weakly. She slid her left hand under the plump little body. Still no reaction. She closed the hand gently and moved the bird into the cage. The gull fluttered weakly as she closed the cover, and then became still again.

"Come on, Sam," she called. "Heel. We're heading for the vet." And off they went to her car, parked on the other side of the house. Sam stalled at the back door, not too eager to make the trip. He associated the word "vet" with sharp needles and prying hands. But, with a helping push on his large hindquarters, he made it up onto the back seat. The bird cage strapped easily into the front seat. The gull had evidently given up any thought of fighting. The car started easily. Charlie backed it out on to the road, and sped for the bridge, doing her best to dodge the bumps. She was concentrating so much on her passenger that she failed to see or hear Mrs. Southerland, who had come out the kitchen door and was yelling at her.

Phil Atmor settled back in his office chair and put his feet up on the desk. The wall clock struck ten. "That's all?"

"That's all." Claudia Sylvia closed her dictation book, stuck her pen into her hair, and smiled at him. "This is the result of your hands-off management. You look tired, Philip."

"I am. Now that we're living in the same house we can do more arguing, but with a heck of a lot less breath."

"Still can't stand the woman, hey?" Claudia pushed her glasses back up on her nose. The light-refracting lenses made it impossible for him to read her expression. Despite the length of time she had been on the job, he would fire her in a second if he thought she was laughing at him. Claudia was sure of that because his father had fired her three times for the same reason. One of the firings had lasted for four days before he'd come around to her house to apologize.

"Worse than that," he grumbled as he swung around to stare out of the windows at the busy harbor. "She's really getting to me."

"Ah."

"What the hell does that mean?"

Claudia shrugged her shoulders. "Oh—just a general comment. You're as jumpy as a flea on a skinny dog. What's the matter?"

"Claudia, you wouldn't believe! My mother's back."

"For a visit, I suppose?" It was time to be gentle. There was nothing bad Claudia could not willingly believe about his mother. Phil flashed her a thankful smile.

"For a *short* visit, I hope." He took a couple of pacing steps across the triple width of the windows. He stopped long enough to rub the back of his neck, and looked at his secretary as if seeing her for the first time. "Why is it, Claudia, that I've grown up thinking that *you* were my mother?"

Claudia Sylvia swung away from him, showing him her back as she dabbed at her eyes. "What a nice thing for you to say, Philip."

"Nice, hell," he muttered. "I'm not a nice person. Would you believe, I just *discovered* that? For years I've considered myself to be a fine all-around fellow."

"And now you know better?"

"And now I know better. Why couldn't my father have married you?"

She ducked her head again and fumbled for a Kleenex. "After your mother ran off," she said softly, "your father still loved her. Almost until the day he died he worshiped her. He just—didn't see *me* as a wife."

"And for what?" he snapped. "She ran off with that damn musician and never gave my dad another thought."

"Musician?"

"Yeah. The first one. The second one, I understand, is an art critic, or something like that."

"What do you suppose she wants, Philip?"

"I don't know," he said, sighing. "But I'm damn sure it'll cost me something. Would you know it? She brought Emily back with her."

"The girl you were engaged to way back then? Don't tell me she went with your mother?"

"No, not with, but at the same time. You'll remember the business was going through a bad patch at that time, and along came Lionel Atwater."

"Good Lord, he must have been thirty years older than she was. And as ugly as sin!"

"All redeemed by the fact that he had three million dollars in the bank, Claudia. Evidently Atwater lost it all, and then had the good spirit to shoot himself. So Emily is looking for another husband.''

"By the name of Atmor?"

"You guessed it." Philip went back to the window, with both hands in his pockets. "She doesn't seem to understand that you can't always grab the brass ring a second time around."

"More than likely she feels she's a *femme fatale*. And so?"

"And so I blandly announced that Charlie and I were going to marry."

"Wonderful! Charlie?" All her mother love was in her voice. She hugged him, and then faltered as he turned around.

"Not so wonderful," he said dolefully. "I seemed to have missed one important part. I forgot to tell Charlie before I made the announcement!"

Claudia shook her head as she squeezed his big hand. "You've just never grown up, Phil, have you? Girls like to be asked. And then she—"

"Blew her top. I never knew there were so many words in the language all meaning 'idiot.' She ranted and raged and promised instant retaliation."

"Well, you've nothing more to do around here. Why don't you go home and make up to her? Take some flowers—some chocolates if she likes them."

"Down-on-my-knees time?"

"You'd better believe it. Want me to call and say you're coming?"

"That would be great, Claudia." He went back behind his desk and settled into his swivel chair, while Claudia dialed the number and said a few words.

"You'd better take this, Philip." She handed the telephone across the desk. "Some woman. Emily something-or-other."

"Freitas." He nodded and took the handset. "I'd like to talk to Charlie," he said. The instrument garbled something at him. "Charlotte MacEnnaly. My fiancée. The little redheaded girl." Another gabble from the other end.

"What the hell do you mean, she's gone? You're sure?" Another gabble of noise came down the wire. "Jesus wept," he muttered as he handed back the handset and Claudia hung it up.

"She's gone," he reported angrily. "Nobody knows where. She just got in her car and zoomed away toward the city. I've got to get out there and see what I can find out."

"Whoa up," Claudia said. "Don't go rushing off half-cocked."

"Why not? That's the only way Charlie and I seem to get along with each other."

He rushed out of the office, struggling to get into his suit jacket, muttering under his breath. One of the arms of the jacket was inverted. As he went through the outer office door he pulled the whole thing off in disgust and threw it at the wastebasket in the corner.

Alice Sturdevent, at her typewriter, stopped and stared. She had never seen her boss in such a condition. Claudia, who had—more than once—picked up the telephone and called the garage to have his car brought around.

And then the very practical businesswoman relaxed her guard and dreamed a little. How much like his father he was, she thought. His hidden strengths came out when he was angry or in crisis. There was not an ounce of his mother in him, thank goodness! After his father had died so tragically Phil had picked up the pieces, and now Atmor Fisheries was ten times as big as it had been. But Phil had paid the price. He had become a confirmed narrow-gauge bachelor, hard-driven by his ambitions.

Charlie? Charlie MacEnnaly. Charlotte Atmor! A nice-sounding name. She might just make a different man out of him. Expand his horizons. That sort of thing. Claudia sighed and went back to her desk. Despite what she had told him, there were a million things that needed to be done.

Traffic was light on the city streets. It was ten-thirty, and everyone who had a job was working at it. Which was fortunate, because Phil Atmor found it hard to keep his mind on his navigation. Too many minor points were in his way. Had he been too firm, too demanding last night? She was not a woman to put up with much domination. You might cajole her into something, but force her? Not a chance.

And the last—happenstance had really got out of hand. When she'd gone into her bedroom the back zip on her blouse had stuck, and since everyone in the house had gone to bed, she'd called on him for help. Nothing wrong with that, of course. It had taken him a little time to break the zip free, and remove the extra thread on which it was caught. But then he'd got carried away with machismo. Both his hands had come around her, almost of their own volition, it had seemed, and gently cupped her breasts. Soft but firm, sweet, they'd felt as they had hardened under his hands. He had been almost hypnotized, and it had taken more than several minutes before he'd realized that *she* wasn't having as good a time as he. She had been, in fact, squirming ineffectually against him, whispering, "No!" in a very firm voice.

When her message had finally got through, he had let her go, only to have her turn on him and swing a hand in the direction of his chin. Her right hand, the one still in a cast. He had snatched the hand before it had hit him, and could not understand why she couldn't understand. He had done it for her. Taken control of her hand in order that she might not hurt her already injured fingers!

So they were at loggerheads again. He, with a perfectly good excuse for *not* letting her use her hand on him, she with a much weaker argument about "not doing what you were doing, you rotten, despicable..."!

Back to square one again, he had pushed her away from him while still controlling both wrists. She hadn't wanted to wake anyone else up by yelling, but she'd been staring at him, mouthing curses, and every now and again trying to kick his shins with her bare foot. So what could any sensible fellow do? He'd pushed her into the over-stuffed chair by her bed, and then run for the door. As he'd closed it behind him something had smashed against the inside of the portal. He could only hope that it wasn't his Meissen shepherdess statuette. The one he had bought in Heidelberg for three hundred dollars.

And there it was. Except for his slight oversight, caressing her breasts, he had done everything with perfect logic. Any woman would have seen that, but not Charlie MacEnnaly. No indeed. Every little infraction of the rules had to be blown up into a monumental crisis. For that matter, the—touching—of her breasts had been a perfectly natural thing for a male of the species to do. Didn't it say in the Bible something about "go forth and multiply"? And didn't God provide a perfectly satisfactory system for multiplication? So now why has she run off into the wild blue?

"Or, for that matter, why am I rushing home as if I had a guilty conscience?" he muttered. "I should have stuck with my pig!"

He put his foot down on the accelerator. Luckily he had already left the highway, and was sashaying down the narrow Neck road, and all the state police were concentrating elsewhere. By the time he drove up beside the house he had almost convinced himself that he was a wronged man. Somebody had left the lawn sprinkler on. Another grievous injury, he thought. He struggled out of the car and ran for the side door, but not fast enough to avoid the sweep of the circular sprinkler.

"Has my clock stopped?" Beth Southerland asked as she heard him come in. "You said one o'clock for lunch."

"So I'm early," he grumbled. "Where is she?"

"Your mother? In the living room, Mr. Atmor. And asking for you time after time."

"I'll get to her some time," he snapped. "Where's Charlie? I called and some idiot told me she'd driven off!"

"I took the call." The voice behind him was chilly enough to make for a very short summer. He turned around just as Beth brought him a kitchen towel to dry himself off.

"You, Emily?"

"Me. That—woman is giving you the business, Philip. I saw her. She wandered off into that house next door, and then when she thought no one was looking she drove off in that Jeep thing. She's up to no good."

"I wouldn't be surprised," he said, and then stopped to think. Charlie was giving him a hard time? Impossible. Charlie was as good as gold. Some little misunderstanding, perhaps, but—a misunderstanding like that one last night? Dear Lord, what have I done? Now if it were Emily I'd think differently. Tall, slender Emily. Blond hair. Was it always blond? He couldn't remember. Little Emily, with the sharp nose and ears so sensitive that they heard every rumor in town. Emily, who stayed with me through thick and thin, for a whole three days after my mother left home. Two days after the stock of Atmor Fisheries dropped ten points. Dear, dependable Emily. Hah!

For something to do while he thought, he used Beth's towel to wipe his face and neck, and then scrubbed at his hair until it was dry. "And who the devil left the sprinkler on?" he asked as he came out from under the towel.

"I don't know," Beth answered. "I was upstairs cleaning the bathroom."

"She did," Emily reported, trying her best to portray righteous indignation. "That fiddler Charlie."

"Violinist," he corrected absentmindedly.

"What difference does it make?" Emily snapped. "Fiddler smiddler. I don't believe she can play a note. What would you expect from a *girl* named *Charlie*? I saw her turn on the sprinkler."

Phil was experiencing that nervous feeling in his stomach again. "You see a lot, Emily," he mused.

"Well, I use my eyes. I don't drift around in a daze, like some women you know. Where are you going?"

"To make a telephone call," he said, and rushed off into the living room. His mother, who had been sitting in an armchair by the fireplace, looked up, saw him, and put down her fashion magazine.

"Philip. You're just in time. I've been worrying about you."

"So have I," he retorted, not really understanding. "We've got to find her."

"We? Who?" The question snapped his head up from the telephone book, and for the first time in many years he really looked at his mother. At five feet nine, he remembered, she was taller than his father by an inch. Time had marked her with little wrinkles around her pale blue eyes. What other ravages there were she had disputed all the way, and covered the ruins of the losing battle with pancake makeup. Her hair was still blond, although a speckle or two of white could be seen close to the roots. She was still as slender as her pictures reminded, but there was an odd bulge or two here and there.

"I have to make an urgent call," he told her.

"And then we'll talk?"

"And then we'll talk." He turned back to the telephone and dialled nine-one-one. The emergency services listened, and finally passed him on to the missing persons bureau of the police department, where a bored detective took down the vital statistics.

"This girl is your fiancée and you don't know her age or when she was born?"

"Look, Detective Silveria, we weren't keeping a score card!"

"But she is five feet six, red hair, green eyes, slender."

"Yeah, and driving a Jeep Wagoneer. This year's model."

"And she's been gone for how long?"

"About eight hours, I guess. I wasn't here when she left."

"You had some kind of an argument with her?"

"Well—not really an argument, but we did have a small...disagreement."

"Look, Mr. Atmor, there's not much we can do until twenty-four hours have elapsed. We have dozens of these missing persons reports every week. What you consider to be a little argument, she may think is a pretty big affair. Hit her, did you? What did you say?"

"You wouldn't want to know," Phil growled. "So you won't do anything for twenty-four hours?"

"I'm afraid not, Mr. Atmor. That's the policy. If you have a picture of her?"

"I don't have a picture," Phil snapped.

"Some fiancée," the detective commented, and hung up. Phil was red-faced from swallowing his words. He wound up like a baseball pitcher, with the telephone in his right fist, and looked for the nearest window.

"Philip?"

The interruption brought him back to common sense. He lowered the telephone gently back on to its cradle, almost as if it were made out of eggshells.

"They're not going to do anything for twenty-four hours? What a queer policy."

"Yes, isn't it, Mother?" His hands were jittering. He wanted badly to choke something or tear something or throw something—almost anything. Why the hell would she run off like that? It was—well, perhaps it was a little spat, but certainly not serious. And if you sit and think about it, he told himself, you'll wind up as a certified loony. Find something to take your mind off Charlie MacEnnaly! He stopped his pacing and sat down, determined to be an executive. His mother profited by his decision; he might well have roared at her as a substitute.

Instead he asked gently, "And what can I do for you, Mother?"

Her hands fluttered in the air. She had a speech already rehearsed, but had forgotten it. "You know that Alfred and I..." she started out. "We have—"

"Alfred? Who the devil is Alfred? The musician?"

"Oh, no." She giggled in a high falsetto. "No, Bernard was the musician. Alfred is a—developer. He and I plan to marry, only he has this tiny problem about developing the land parcel he owns in Majorca."

"That's what I'm best at," he said, sighing. "Little problems. Just for the hell of it, what happened to Bernard?"

"Oh, he proved to be totally unsuitable." His tall, proud mother hastily snatched a tiny wisp of a cambric handkerchief from her purse and dabbed at her eyes.

"That's what Dad said," Phil commented.

"Don't, Phil. You have no idea about your father. He was ruthless, cruel—"

"And very dead," Phil said. "I remember that part. And all the time I thought he was a fairly good man. Would you believe that?"

His mother took one good look at his stern face and took refuge in her handkerchief again.

"So tell me about your little problem," he continued.

"Well, it's only a little thing," his mother told him. "Lots of little regulations and papers and things like that before Alfred can begin building."

"I'm beginning to see," Phil said. "The little thing is money?"

"Yes. Just a little bit, and Alfred said that surely my son could help us out?"

"Yes, I'm sure Alfred would say that," he replied. "Just how much is a little?"

"I—hardly anything at all," she said. And then, very hesitantly, "One hundred thousand?"

"Pesetas?"

"Dollars." She shrank into her chair as he stood up, his lips working. What he might have said, however, had to wait for another day. Now, what with one thing and another, it was almost six o'clock in the evening. He had spent a full working day just worrying. A car came thumping over the floating bridge, stirred up a dust cloud on the dirt road, and wheeled to a stop next to his in the driveway.

Phil didn't wait to see who would get out. He ran for the door like a madman, burst out into the yard, and came upon Charlie as if she were a rich relative reported long dead.

"Hey!" she yelled as he gathered her in with his hands around her tiny waist and swung her around in a big circle before depositing her on the ground.

"Lord," he murmured in her ear as he hugged her with a great deal of enthusiasm. "I thought you'd run off." Charlie started to answer, but could not squeeze a word out from around his kissing lips. That was the moment that Sam, caught in the back seat, gave up trying to work the door lock and started to squeal for help. "Oh, hell," Phil said as he set Charlie aside and unlatched the door.

"Now, where were we?" His hand reached for her waist and lifted her off the ground. "I remember that part," he said solemnly, "and then," he swung her around one more time and lowered her to the ground, "and then what?"

"This," she told him as she threw her arms around his neck and stretched up high enough to kiss him.

"Yeah, now I remember." His hands took control, his lips seduced her, and he shivered as her softness worked its magic everywhere.

They both ran out of breath at the same time. The exercise came to a regrettable end, and she giggled at him. "Yes, that's the way I remember it."

Phil took a deep breath, Sam nudged his leg, and he remembered all his grievances, big and little. All the anxiety, all the fear, the police report—and she even took my pet pig with her! he told himself angrily.

"Look, Charlotte MacEnnaly," he growled. "Just where the hell have you been?"

CHAPTER SIX

IT WAS like a man lighting a match to see if he had any gas in his tank. Charlie exploded. "Where the hell have I been? Who the hell are you to ask me where the hell I've been?" Charlie glared up at him. He glared back. Sam scuttled for cover.

"I've been on an errand of mercy," she said icily from the other side of the car.

"And I've been calling the police and the fire department and all the emergency services for the last eight hours, worrying my head off. What do you have to say to that?"

Wrong question, wrong person. She gave him the short answer. "Goodbye." And then she turned on her heel, went back to her car, and drove it around to the other side of her house. The gull's box had been approved and padded by the veterinarian. Charlie managed to manhandle it around the corner and into the house, where she set the cage up next to her fireplace. The nurse had given the bird some sort of a sedative shot, while the vet had examined the wing and splinted it.

"A difficult bird to house," the vet told her. "You could leave him here with me if you'd like."

"I'm not working," Charlie told him, "and I know your prices. I couldn't afford it."

"So I'll have my son carry him back to the car. Here's a list of treatment instructions. Make sure he has plenty of water." And so they had come home in a hurry, because she didn't want to be late for Phil. Who had promptly said—what he had said, and ruined a fine happy day.

There was a thump on her door. She went over and opened it a crack. Sam sat anxiously outside, wagging that little excuse for a tail.

Like owner like pig, Charlie told herself. "Go home," she commanded, and waved her hand in the general direction of the other house. "Go join that rotten friend of yours." Sam looked puzzled. "Go," she repeated, just a little louder. Looking as if he couldn't believe it, Sam backed off the porch and waddled his way back around the fence.

"So there," Charlie said. And why did I do that? You can't blame a clean decent pig for the errors of its master, she thought, and started toward the door. But by the time she got there Sam was out of sight.

Disgruntled, both at Phil and herself, Charlie wandered back to the kitchen and scanned the shelves. Campbell's beans in tomato sauce. The only one-can meal she could possibly fix. She shook her head and looked further, but there was nothing else available. She took down the can and set it next to her electric can-opener. "Toast and beans," she muttered. "Lord, why are you doing this to me?" There was a pounding at her door.

"Sam again," she said, and then yelled, "Okay, I'm coming. I'll compromise if I have to." She threw the door open without looking. "All right, Sam. Come in. I don't have a thing to eat but..." The man standing at her door grinned. He had been Charlie's agent for almost eight years, and nothing could surprise him.

"James," she squeaked. She threw her hands around his neck, kissed his cheek, and pulled him into the house.

"Well, now that's what an agent needs," he said. "A real welcome."

"And what brings you here, James?" She gave him another enthusiastic kiss. James Terwiller, one of the most pleasant musical agents in the country, was not quite six feet tall, with a rotund figure. With his hat on he looked to be a youthful twenty-five or thirty. Only when he doffed it could one see his fringe of white hair, and gauge his proper age, in the fifties.

"I haven't heard from my favorite violinist," he said. "And, with the performance in Boston due in two weeks, I thought I might as well come down to check up. And what in the name of Mozart have you done to your hand?" He reached out and corralled her right hand. "May the Lord bless us!" he exclaimed. "Bruised? Bent?"

She pulled her hand back and tucked it behind her back. "Broken," she admitted.

"Good heavens!"

"You didn't know?" He shook his head. "But— Phil was supposed to call you. He said he *had* called you. And you didn't hear a word?"

"Not a word," James replied. "This is quite a shock, Charlie. Let me check my notebook." He sprawled out into her captain's chair and ran his eyes over several pages. "When will you be able to play again?"

"Three weeks—perhaps," she reported. "If I'm lucky."

"Maybe I can get Maria Schuster," he muttered as he paged through his book. "Yes, Maria." Without asking permission he picked up Charlie's telephone and dialed a long-distance number. Charlie leaned against the table and listened shamelessly.

Yes, Maria was available. Yes, Maria knew the Tchaikovsky number. Yes, Maria appreciated this would be her big break, playing with the symphonic, and she would be forever grateful to her lovable James.

And yes, Charlie told herself, it would have been my big break, too, and now it's all gone down the tube and I'll get a bad name in the business as being unreliable. And that rotten—man didn't even remember to call in, and left me hanging out to dry! Damn!

"Thank goodness," James announced, "Maria is available, is prepared, and would be glad to oblige her dear friend Charlotte."

"I'll bet she would," Charlie muttered. She knew the figures. There were perhaps ten thousand technically qualified violin soloists in the world, give or take a thousand, and in any average week only forty-seven of them could expect to be employed. It didn't really matter how good your *last* performance was, all the impresarios wanted to know was "What can you do for me now?" And if all you could answer was, "I had to decline because I broke my finger while trying to slap a pig-man," you had used up all your goodwill in one fell swoop.

"I'm glad I came," James said as he tucked his notebook back into his inside coat pocket. "A day or two more and I would have been in the soup. And don't worry, Charlie. Nobody plays as well as you do. I'll start hunting you up another performance—say in five or six weeks?"

She knew he meant well but could not produce. James was a lovable, bumbling man, well qualified in the field of music, who always looked for the sunny side of life—and only occasionally found it.

"Yes, I know," she told him. "I'll count on it."

He winced, shrugged his shoulders, and had another thought. "You're really out in the boondocks, Charlotte. I couldn't find a motel anyplace around, and it's getting a little late in the day. I don't suppose you . . . ?"

"Put you up?" He smiled in relief. "Of course, you'll have to bed down on the couch."

"At my age, the couch?"

Charlie shook her head and chuckled. "You never give up, do you, James. A man your age? I would think you'd be glad to have the couch."

"I'm not *that* old," he grumbled. "But, if that's all that's going, I'll be happy to sleep on the couch. Now, about dinner?"

"That I can provide," she said, chuckling. "I'd already decided to have it myself, and I'm sure we can stretch it for two. Toast and beans. How's that sound?''

Charlie had a hard time suppressing her grin. James's face was so easy to read. Which might be the reason, she thought, that so many really great deals got away from him.

"Beans?"

"And toast," she assured him. "Very healthy. Plenty of protein. Of course, if you want something more prosaic, there's a fairly good restaurant just a couple of miles from here."

He leaped for the substitution. "Done. Dutch treat, of course."

"The last of the big-time spenders," she said, chuckling. "Give me a few minutes to freshen up, and we'll go."

Charlie had intended to comb her hair, splash a little water on her face, and redo her lipstick. Just enough to satisfy James. But, as she stood in front of her mirror and tried to brush her hair with her left hand, another thought burst. Dress for James? No, no indeed. Dress to get back at that—monster next door. Let him eat his heart out!

So she stripped to the essentials, struggled into her tight blue sweater, added a short wraparound skirt which terminated at mid-thigh, and did her best to put her hair up—to no avail. One-handed hairdressing was definitely out. She shook her head in disgust, brushed her hair out again, and stood back to watch as her natural curls reestablished their control.

James was a little impatient, Charlie noticed, and she had only been three quarters of an hour. She handed him the little pearl necklace that her grand-mother had left for her. "Fasten this, James?"

"Good Lord, is this some hoity-toity place we're going to?"

"Not really," she assured him. "A nice place, but not fancy. Can you get that catch to fasten?"

"In my day I've fastened thousands of them," he boasted, and then was suddenly sobered by the amount of history he was revealing. He gave the catch one more inspection. "Why do I have the impression that you're not dressing for me?"

"Pure imagination," she said as she took his arm. From next door she had just heard the back door slam. Sam was out and about. "Shall we go?"

"Isn't it a little early for dinner?"

"No, Lord, no," she replied. "It has to be still daylight."

He gave her another one of those questioning looks. "We have to have daylight to eat? What sort of a res-taurant is this?"

"Nothing like that," she lied. "It's just that—well, the bridge is always a problem, and there are no streetlights in these parts, so I want to be sure we get back safely. Surely you understand?"

"Of course," James returned. "I think."

She urged him to the door and out, then took back her working hand in order to give her door a good slam. Sam, rooting around by his own back door, gave a little squeal and trotted toward the end of the fence line.

"Door stuck?" James asked as she took his arm again and steered him toward that same fence.

"Warped," she commented. "Something to do with the spring rains and like that." Sam, who was gauging their movement, worked himself up to high speed to be sure they would meet wherever she was going. As a result, the pig had to put on his brakes and almost skidded into them.

"What the—?" James, one of the last brave men out of his century, maneuvered so that Charlie was between him and the pig. "What in the world is that?"

He had reason for worry. Sam was a very possessive pig, who recognized in a flash that *his* girlfriend was stepping out with the wrong man. So he assumed his pointer position, with his flat muzzle almost on James's thigh, and he grumbled. And he grunted. And finally, getting no success, he squealed in rage.

"Hey," James protested as he backed off a foot or two. Behind them, the door of Phil's house slammed. Very satisfactory, Charlie thought. She maneuvered them until James's back was toward Phil's house.

"Don't mind him," she assured her agent. "That's Sam. He's a mini-pig."

"He doesn't look very mini to me," James protested. "He looks to be a whole lot of pig. A boar? Look at the size of those teeth! A bad-tempered pig, he sounds like."

"He's only teasing," Charlie told him. "He wouldn't hurt a baby."

"Babies I don't worry about," James retorted. "How is he with adults?"

Sam had been listening intently. He knew few of the words, but recognized the tone. And this was definitely one dude who shouldn't be squiring Charlie around. He could feel the aura of fear. So why not add on? the pig thought. He struggled to raise himself up on hind legs, balanced his forelegs against James's belt line, and gave a massively bad-tempered squeal.

James almost jumped out of his skin. He moved hastily behind Charlie again, which was the wrong signal to be giving to Sam. The pig emitted a grumbling roar and tried to catch up.

"Down, Sam!" The command came from Phil Atmor, who had come up behind them. The pig dropped to the ground and held his position. Phil glared at all three of them. His face was so red that Charlie thought he might choke himself to death. It gave her a delightful feeling. She moved out in front of Sam and took a deep breath—and held it in.

There was no doubt in her mind that Phil was looking in the right direction—just below her chin. And he was not enjoying it at all—or was he? Unfortunately Charlie ran out of breath before her silhouette achieved its maximum potential. She flashed one of her innocent little smiles.

"James," she said, "this is Mr. Atmor, my next-door neighbor. And his pet pig, Sam."

"A pleasure," James acknowledged, and reached out a hand. Phil looked as if there was no pleasure at all in the meeting. He jammed both hands into his pant pockets and glared at them. Sam, feeling the tide of emotion, and wanting to be on the right side, sat down on his broad hindquarters and squealed again.

Charlie, her mission accomplished, took James's arm again and tugged him out toward the road, where he had left his car.

"Not too pleasant a fellow," James commented as they moved away.

"No," Charlie replied, a little more loudly than the conversation required. "He tends to be a grouch—a dog in the manger."

"A pig in the manger," James corrected.

"Very clever," Charlie said, adding a little artificial tinkle of amusement. "A very difficult neighbor."

"And only two houses on the island?"

"Only two," she replied mournfully. "I'm afraid nothing will help until one of us moves."

"You may need a good local lawyer," James advised. "I have a brother with a law office over on Union Street in the city. Here's his card. Tell him I sent you—he'll give a discount."

James seated her in his rental car, and went around to the driver's side. Charlie, feeling that her mission had been accomplished, threw a little more gasoline on the fire. She leaned over and bussed James on the cheek, and then waved to Phil as they drove down toward the bridge. A *very* satisfactory evening, she told herself. Eat that, monster man!

CHAPTER SEVEN

CHARLIE was up early the next morning. James was a champion snorer, rocking the house with his serenade. Their evening meal had been mediocre, the wine suffered from quantity instead of quality, and the service was terrible. On the way back James had tried to put a move on her. It had stirred her guilty conscience more than her anger. She was using him, blatantly using him. So, rather than slap his face, she had lifted his arm from her shoulder and moved to the far side of the car.

He'd wanted coffee when they'd reached her house. Charlie had regretted she had invited him to stay the night, but her conscience would not allow her to weasel out of her promise. She'd wanted a night of uninterrupted sleep, so when she'd poured *his* coffee into a big mug she had added two liberal doses of brandy to it, and Mr. Wolf had spent the night on her sofa, playing Sweet Little Lamb.

There was one thing more Charlie wanted to milk out of this situation. She was up before James, and made him a breakfast of toast and coffee and orange juice, all the while remaining in her cotton nightgown. The gown flowed all the way down to her ankles. It was as transparent as a pair of sunglasses being worn outdoors on a moonless night. But from the outside it had all the look of a sexy garment.

"I'm not in all that much of a hurry," James said as she pushed him through the meal, back into his shoes, and out the door. Sam, an early riser, was waiting at her door.

"Move over, Sam." The pig reluctantly moved. James seemed to be having some problem with his eyes and head. Surely two shots of brandy can't do that? Charlie thought. Well, they were pretty big shots, come to think of it. So she ducked under James's arm, helped rest his weight on her tiny shoulders, and assisted him out to his car. Out of the corner of her eyes Charlie could see the movement of the lace curtains in Phil's living room window.

After James had driven off, promising to get himself something quickly for his "headache," Charlie stood in the middle of the road for a time, then turned around toward Phil's house and stretched mightily. The lace curtain dropped back into place. "Take that," she muttered to the wide, wide world as she strolled back to her own house and slammed the door behind her. And, for some unaccountable reason, she started crying.

The side door shook as if the Big Bad Wolf were assaulting it for the third time in one day. Charlie, dressed and safely huddled on the bed in her own house, put up with it for five more minutes, and then walked over to the door. She sniffed a couple of times, and grabbed at a Kleenex to dry her eyes. "Go away," she yelled through the panel. "Smart pig? Hah! You live next door, pig, not here!"

The assault continued. "Now I know why his last housekeeper quit on him," she muttered as she went into the kitchen for her broom. With her weapon at the ready, tucked under her right arm, she flipped the handle on her new lock and the door flew open. It wasn't Sam banging on the door; it was his master.

"What the devil do *you* want here?" She looked up into his craggy face and stepped back a couple of paces. "Keep your distance," she threatened. For once he did, leaning casually against the frame of her screen door and trying his best to look pleasant.

"You wanted something? Come in my door and I'll bash you with my broom," she threatened under her breath. He must have heard at least one of the words.

"I'm trying to be neighborly," he complained. "Do you use that broom for sweeping or riding?"

"So that's neighborly?" She glared at him. Her beautiful red hair swung around in front of her face. She had to drop the broom in order to brush it aside. "First you insult me, then you cripple me. You do me out of earning my living, and now you call me a witch. That was what you implied, wasn't it? *Witch?*" At the end of each statement her voice rose an octave, until the last witchery was a scream of real indignation.

"Hold on now," he said, trying to calm her down. "Let's start again."

"Yes," she snapped. "It won't improve things, but then, things can't get any worse than they are." He nodded his head a couple of times, and knocked on her already open door. Lord, she sighed to herself,

look at the size of those hands. He could break me
into little pieces—or hug me until I had to cry quits!
Her cheeks turned red, and he noticed. That big happy
grin came across his face. "So say something," she
added.

"Hello. How are you this morning?"

"I'm mad as a wet hen," she snapped at him.
"Your damn—pet thinks I'm going to provide hand-
outs for him four times a day. Don't you have some
women over at your house who could look after
him?"

"But you told me Sam needed a diet." Said innocently in that tone that the devil used to snatch good
souls away!

"So it's my fault? I've resigned the job, Mr. Atmor.
You can take care of your own stupid animal. There
isn't enough room on this island for the two of us,
never mind your pig!" Somehow or another her left
hand balled up into a fist, but she dared not swing it.
She might hit him and have *two* broken hands.

"That's what I've come to complain about, Miss
MacEnnaly. Did you know that state law prohibits
trapping and caging wild birds?"

"No, I didn't know that," she snapped back at him.
"Blame it on my low grades in school. So who's—
whatever you just said?"

"I think it's quite obvious, ma'am. Just outside
your door is a cage, and inside the cage is a herring
gull. You're not going to tell me the bird trapped itself?"

"Ma'am? I'm not your darn mother!"

"My mistake. You've certainly changed," he said mournfully. "There are specks of white in your hair, and wrinkles around your eyes. You're growing old fast, lady. Hey!"

But Charlie MacEnnaly had gone, making a mad dash for the big mirror in her bedroom. After a careful examination she came back out again, steaming. "Lies. All lies," she shouted at him. "Even a mother couldn't love somebody like you!"

"The gull?" he asked in sweet innocence.

"Don't you give me that, you—man! I told you some time ago that he had a broken wing and I took him to the veterinarian to have a splint put on him, and all you did *then* was to bluster and yell like some kid with his favorite toy broken. Well, the situation's still the same. Hank still has a broken wing, and he's going to stay here until it gets better. Have you got that all written down? If you want a phone to call the police you can use mine." She stepped aside and waved an arm for him to enter.

"No, I don't think so. You might have some trap, or try to compromise me, or something. My mother's been warning me about girls like you."

"I'll bet she has. Did you get your ring back? I stuffed it in your letter slot!"

"You know, I'm beginning to believe you *did* go to the vet's. Maybe it was all a mistake. I'm sure I didn't bluster. I admit I was perhaps a little loud-spoken, but you deserved it! You could have told someone where you were going, instead of barging off into the wide blue. Come on back to my house, Charlie. I'll forgive you and we'll forget it all, right?"

"*You'll* forgive *me*? You're crazy—has all that fish oil melted your mind? I'm willing to forget—if you'll move away some place. I hear there are some fine houses available in Pago Pago. Goodbye."

"Now that's enough, Charlie. You're only driving your blood pressure up out of range. You know darn well you can't take care of yourself. What did you have for breakfast?"

"Toast. Two pieces. I made three but your damn—your animal ate one of them."

"No orange juice? No coffee? No eggs? What kind of a meal is that for a growing girl? Look at you. You've lost five pounds at least. And right where you can't afford it!" He had walked into the kitchen by this time, and patted the outward curve of her hips. "Look at that," he mourned. "Five pounds at least, and up here—" His hands wandered upward.

"Don't you dare!" she snapped, backing away from him. In her haste she forgot where the footstool was located, and backed right over it, to come down on her broadest proportion with a terrific thud. It hurt. "Now look what you've done," she groaned. But I won't cry. I'm never going to let this man see me crying, she told herself, not ever again.

"Aren't you going to help me up?" She glared at him and gingerly tested her landing area.

"No, I don't think so," he told her. "You might hurt me or something. Why don't you just roll over and come up on your hands and knees, love?"

"I've not ever seen a man so concerned about my pains," she gasped as she tried to roll over. "Oh, Lord! My knee!"

He was down beside her in an instant, all his teasing done. He tested her left knee with gentle hands. I suppose they have a course in knee feeling at Harvard, she thought, but it was rather—pleasant, so she swallowed the words.

"You can't get around on that for a while," he announced. "I *told* you you couldn't take care of yourself."

"It's all a lie," she said gruffly. "And all your fault as well."

"Maybe you'd prefer to tell me about that man who took you out last night?"

I *knew* it, she told herself. He *did* watch out of the windows. I saw the curtain fluttering in the rain, and I'm not going to tell him a thing. Watch me, Philip Atmor, as I clam up on you. Along with a haughty expression!

"What a haughty expression you're wearing," he said. But he was laughing at the time he said it, which made Charlie only a slight bit more angry than before. "I take it you aren't going to tell me why he was invited to spend the night?"

"Oh, you noticed?" she muttered. "Please go away."

"Well, my father never raised any dumb kids," he said dolefully. "You obviously don't like me. You specifically asked me to leave. You're not interested in *my* interest. You don't need any help. You'd rather bed the traveling salesman than share time and space with a nice guy like me. I get the message. Goodbye, Miss MacEnnaly."

He stretched upward to the limit of his long legs, brushed off the knees of his pants and stared down at her. "Yes, all true," she muttered. And if you believe that I've got some Confederate money I'd like to sell you, she thought. Why am I so uncomfortable with all this exchange? He is the villain of the piece, not me.

Philip offered a mournful smile and headed for the door. Charlie rocked back and forth for a painful moment, and tried to get up. Her knee protested vigorously. She had to fight back the scream of pain. But when she tried to put all her weight on both feet another sharp pain in her knee overwhelmed her. She dropped into the nearest chair and yelled.

"Phil! Mr. Atmor!" Two seconds later he popped the door open and came in, looking very solemn. Look at him, she told herself through the pain. He was standing outside the darn door, just waiting for me to...!

"You called?"

Tears. They struggled to come, and she fought against them. If he sees just one tear, she told herself, my goose is cooked. So instead she sniffed a time or two and rubbed a knuckle under her eyes.

"Mr. Atmor..." Royally done, if a little stiff. He nodded an acknowledgment. "I—don't seem to be able to walk."

"Ah. Too bad." There was not a slightest sign in his eye concerning mercy, and gallant knights, and all that sort of thing. "Perhaps you'd like me to call the ambulance service."

"No. Of course I don't want you to call the ambulance!" she snapped pettishly. She brushed her hair out of her eyes again and peered up at him warily.

"I see. Can it be, perhaps, that you were wrong? You *do* want me to help? I'm really not as bad as you first thought?"

Charlie took a deep breath, and almost choked on her own choler. It was bad enough for him to be proven right, but to have to admit that she was wrong was more than her stomach could stand. But there was no alternative. Any old port in a storm, she thought. Sitting up in a chair all night didn't appeal.

"I—suppose perhaps I might have been just a slight bit hasty," she offered.

"Only suppose?" She missed the gentle teasing in his voice, her own anger overriding everything.

"I was wrong," she murmured. "I was very wrong. I need your help!" And if you say another word, Phil Atmor, I'm going to murder you!

He must have read her mind, for he said nothing at all. He stooped over her and swept her up into his arms, jiggling her slightly to readjust her weight, squashing her breasts against his cable-muscled chest. "Not a word," she whispered to herself. "Especially no remarks about how I've not lost as much weight as you thought originally. Not a word!"

So they made the trip across the grass, around the chain-link fence, and over to the side of his house, where he kicked at the door. Emily finally came to open it.

"Why, Philip! Whatever has happened?" Hellfire, Charlie thought, I even hate her voice. Why should that be? It's a little shrill, but only so much that a trained musician might have noticed. Besides, she's too skinny. Men like pulchritudinous women like me. Like me? Hah!

"Charlie's had another accident," he said, brushing by Emily and heading toward the couch in the living room. He set her down gently, then lifted her legs up onto the soft pillows. Sam appeared from wherever pigs hid when they wanted to be alone, and sniffed at Charlie's ankles.

"Another accident? The woman seems accident-prone, Philip. You'd better keep your distance."

"Thank you, Emily. I don't think it's contagious." It sounded very little like a real thank-you statement. In fact, because Charlie *wanted* it to sound sarcastic, it did. And meanwhile her good Sir Galahad was sliding her skirt up—well, almost up to *there*, and her hand flashed down to stop the invasion. He knocked it away.

"I have to see what's what," he told her sternly, and his hand returned to its work. "I've seen women's legs before, you know."

Emily tittered; Charlie blushed fiery red. "That's a long way above my knee," she muttered. "It's the knee that hurts." But every time she moved to tug her skirt down he stopped her.

"Swollen," he commented. "I guess we'd better put an ice pack on it. Where else does it hurt?"

What does he take me for? Charlie asked herself. If I tell him where the rest of me hurts and he wants to put an ice pack on my... Oh, no you don't, Mr. Atmor.

"Nothing," she said, sighing. He looked at her skeptically. "Honestly, it doesn't hurt anyplace at all. Not anyplace."

"Yeah," he snorted. "You'd break your back sooner than take my help, wouldn't you? Emily, watch her while I go find the ice pack. Or maybe I should call Mrs. Southerland."

"She's gone home," Emily answered wistfully. "Left a half hour ago. I don't mind helping out. I'd do anything for you, Phil." The pair of them headed for the kitchen, she hugging his arm as they went.

"Yeah, I'll do anything for you," Charlie muttered, imitating the high-pitched saccharine flavor of Emily's comment. "I'll kiss your foot, with or without the shoe. I'll bust your head open with a shovel!" And then Charlie groaned. She wanted very badly to change places with Emily. It was too late in the game to change her character, and she was coming to realize that. He was a *good* man. Well, perhaps not actually good, but how about—acceptable? Maybe even a little more than that. He's too good a man to fall among the Emilys of this world! He'd be much better off if he picked a Charlotte to be his wife! To be his wife? What a crazy thought! She groaned again as Emily came back with the ice pack and a towel.

"We're out of ice," the blonde announced cheerfully as she picked up Charlie's injured leg and shoved the towel beneath it. "Phil has gone into town to get some more."

"Good Lord," Charlie snapped as the pain struck her in waves. "I'm not just a chunk of beef, you know."

"Oh, are you not?" The titter again that jangled Charlie's teeth. "One mustn't let the melted ice ruin Philip's lovely couch, you know." The ice pack slammed down hard on top of the injured knee, just to emphasize that there was nothing accidental going on.

"No, of course one mustn't," Charlie muttered, and added a few words from three of the six foreign languages she knew.

It was evident that Emily's language lore was limited. She smiled and stepped back from the couch, saying, "Now there. Isn't that nice?"

"Yeah. Nice."

"You know, Miss MacEnnaly, you're wasting your time, and you're going to wreck your body with this approach."

"Do you say so?" Charlie groaned as she tried to shift her position. Emily smiled as if she enjoyed the whole affair.

"See for yourself," Emily said happily. "You managed to get his attention by breaking your finger. That didn't last, although you're still left with a cast. So when you saw him drifting back to me you broke your knee." She leaned forward in her chair, and the laughter disappeared. "What do you propose to break when *that* doesn't work?"

"Ah, is that what it is? Philip belongs to you? I didn't know that."

"Of course. You haven't been connected with the Atmor family as long as I have. Why, Phil and I shared the same bathtub when we were children."

And perhaps you still do, Charlie thought glumly. Or bed. Or shower. What's the matter with me? Why do I have this crazy itch? I know what I could break next. Emily's neck! That would be a worthwhile contribution to the culture of the world. If I weren't a lady I'd spit!

But, since she *was* a lady, she held back. "I didn't know," she offered. "It must have been a wonderful childhood. I envy you."

"And so you should. Look." Emily commanded her attention. On her left hand a lovely ring sparkled. Charlie needed only a second or two to recognize that it was the same ring *she* had worn while faking her engagement to Philip, the one she had stuck through his mail slot in a fit of anger. It had felt so good, that ring. The only one she had ever owned. Violinists earned a good salary, but not all *that* good. By the time they were old enough to afford to buy themselves a ring, they were too old to *wear* rings. She stared at Emily, hoping that the other woman would go away.

But cheerful Emily was not about to exit, stage right. Instead she pulled up a chair and settled down in front of Charlie, who had no way to escape. And she picked up a dangerous weapon—two knitting needles—and began to work. "Yeah, look at that," Charlie muttered under her breath. And I can't even sew on a button. I suppose we're going to maintain this lovable domestic scene until after Phil comes back?

"You know," Emily said as her fingers flew back and forth, "Phil and I were born in the same year, but I'm actually a month older than he is."

"Is that a fact?"

"Yes, and it's been one of our humorous little jokes. One of those family things. Once a year, for a month, I'm actually a year older than him!"

"Yeah, very funny. It doesn't seem to bother him, loving an older woman?"

The knitting needles stopped. "It's a joke," Emily said. A sour look flashed across her face. "A family joke. I knew you wouldn't understand. We of the First Families of Massachusetts use little teasers like that to establish bonds."

"I *do* understand," Charlie commented.

Charlie tried to shift her weight. Her knee was damaged, no doubt about that, but her fundament was certainly in no good shape either. The movement brought a painful reminder. She groaned. Her delightful companion looked up from her work and smiled.

"God's own punishment," Emily said.

"Has anybody ever mentioned they'd like to strangle you?" Charlie asked.

"Perhaps, when I was younger," her tormentor continued. "But then, I've been married. I learned a great deal from my first husband. Unfortunately, he lost all his money. It's hard to be a poor widow."

"Not as bad as being an unemployed violinist," Charlie returned bitterly. "I'd like to—"

"There you all are," Phil's mother interrupted as she came down the stairs, all smiles. "I just had to tell somebody, so I wrote immediately to my husband. Oh, he'll be so pleased.''

"You mean that Philip is going to advance the money?'' Emily looked like a woman who owned a cake and found someone else stealing a slice.

"I mean exactly that,'' Mrs. Atmor said gleefully. "Of course, it's a business deal, you understand. Philip will send one of his auditors over, and one of his architect friends. But of course he'll find nothing to be concerned about. Isn't that wonderful? I believe I'll go straight home to Majorca tomorrow. Will you come, dear Emily?''

"No, I think I'll stay on for a time. There are still some—things that Philip and I have to clear up. Like that—pig, for example.''

"I can see how living with a pig could be a difficulty,'' his mother agreed. "Of course, you could always wait until Phil goes on a trip, then take the—animal off to a slaughterhouse.''

"Charming idea. But I don't think I could deliver such a monster. Do you suppose they make house calls?''

"You lay a finger on my—on his pig and your life won't be worth a C sharp,'' Charlie interjected. Sam, who recognized a life-or-death debate when he heard one, sidled down the side of the couch and rested his nose in Charlie's hand. And that was the moment when the ambulance pulled up in front of the house, just behind Phil's Porsche, and the men clomped into the house with their folded stretcher in hand.

Sam immediately deserted, looking for a stronger protector. "It's all right, Sam. Everything's okay,''

Phil said. "Can you guys move her without breaking her leg?"

"Don't worry about it," the leading paramedic said. He came over to the couch and made a quick examination of Charlie's knee.

"I told you I didn't want any ambulance," she muttered as Phil came over to enjoy the show. "Just some ice, that's all I need."

"That's a nasty twist," the paramedic commented. "If nothing's broken inside you'll still need two or three days of bed rest."

"So get her out of here to the hospital," Phil said. "She's hurting. Anybody can see that."

"I've got just the thing right here," the second paramedic said as he whipped out the longest needle Charlie had ever seen.

"I can't stand thunderstorms," Charlie moaned, "or needles."

"You'll never feel a thing," the paramedic said. And his promise came true. Before he could get the needle close to the right place for the injection Charlie squeaked a tiny squeak and fainted.

"So the doctor says that there's nothing broken, and only a bad sprain. I've been here four days—he says I can go home tomorrow if I'm careful. On crutches, I'm afraid, but I hate hospitals. Do you realize how irritating it is to stare at those green walls? Do you realize that there's a crack in the ceiling, and if you look at it long enough it seems to be a fishing boat on the Grand Banks?"

"I'm glad for you," Phil Atmor said in that gentle voice that he normally reserved for pigs and children. "Glad that you're ready to come out of hospital. I'll come get you tomorrow, shall I?"

"I—I would be pleased," Charlie said. "I thought maybe you weren't coming."

"Hey, never say that," he replied. "I've had a little . . . problem—"

"Or two," she interrupted. Her eyes twinkled. He grinned back at her.

"Or two," he agreed. "But my mother decided to go back to Spain, and I managed to get her on the plane last night."

"Please, sit down and tell me about it, Philip. Do I gather that you succumbed?"

"After all, she *is* my mother. It's true she hasn't worked at it for almost fourteen years, but she *is* my mother."

Charlie could not help but look him over. Still tall, rangy, a little thinner than a man that size might have been. His dark eyes gleamed. There was still a little furrow across his brow. "Fish not biting?" she asked.

"Not exactly. Lots of fish, but lots of storms at sea. Some of our boats need overhauls in this summer season. Things like that. If it weren't for Captain Hardy taking over fleet direction I'd be up a creek. Why are you smirking like that?"

"Because something else has happened." She held up her right hand. Her cast had been reduced again. She wiggled her thumb and forefinger, wagged her little finger. "I can feel. I don't know about bowing, but the nurse loaned me a yardstick yesterday and I

was able to handle it. I'm so excited about getting back
to my music that my stomach keeps rolling over.''

"Damn," he said.

"Damn?"

"I'm afraid you might want to be up and about
your fiddling—er—violining," he murmured. "You're
like some sort of butterfly."

"That beautiful?" The sigh was satisfaction. This
was the sort of conversation she could dabble with for
hours and hours.

"No, because I can't pin you down," he said
gruffly. "Next thing I know you'll be off to Boston, or
Vienna, or—"

"Oshkosh," she interrupted. "That's dumb, Phil.
I'll have to practice for hours and hours and hours
before I can play in concert again." He relaxed in his
chair and the worry lines faded just the slightest.

"Oshkosh?"

"It's a nice place," she told him. "Now tell me what
sort of a game you played on your mother."

"Who, me? You think I might try to bamboozle my
own mother?"

"Yes," she said, and a wicked little grin expanded
to fill her whole face.

"Nagger. So, all right, the deal wasn't as simple as
it sounds. She convinced me that this ought to be a
business deal, complete with investigations, proper
financing, contracts. You know."

"*She* convinced you?"

"O, ye of little faith," he grumbled. "So I'm send-
ing out a couple of investigators, my chief account-
ant, and a land specialist. All these people will file a

report, and if they approve I shall loan my mother one hundred and fifty thousand dollars.''

''And how much of a chance does your mother have?''

''About as much as a snowball surviving overnight in Hell. As it happens, I've already started the investigation. It now appears that her new husband is well known among the police forces of the Riviera. I seriously doubt he can even remain out of jail for another four weeks.''

''Phil! Your own mother! Disgraceful.''

''Yes, isn't it?''

Charlie stopped to think this over. If I *had* a mother I'd darn well treat her better than that, she told herself. A woman who sacrificed all her—well, *some* of her life to him, and he... But one hundred and fifty thousand dollars—that ain't exactly hay, is it?

''What are you thinking about,'' he asked. ''My mother?''

She nodded.

''You haven't met my mother,'' he told her. ''She's also my secretary, and my father's secretary before me. Claudia has taken care of me for years and years. I think maybe I'll enter her as Mother of the Year.''

''And if *she* asked you for that amount of money?''

''I'd give her the keys to my safe-deposit box.'' And with that he leaned over her bed and kissed her as soundly as was possible for a man who was not allowed to lean on the patient's bed, couldn't find a place to hang on to the patient, and was an enthusiastic kisser.

"Good Lord," she gasped when it finally came to a halt.

"Yeah," he agreed, mopping his brow. "Is this the way you handle all your men friends?"

"I can't remember," she half whispered. "He was only ten years old. And how about Sam and your girlfriend?"

"Sam's great, and *you're* my girl!"

"That's not the way I heard it." Charlie tendered a little glare. A very little glare. Somehow it no longer seemed politic or pleasant to rant and rave at him. "What does *she* want, as if I didn't know?"

"Well, if you know, you'd better tell me," he said wryly. "All she does is sit around and tell me about how it was in the old days, and then she cries at me."

"Why in the world would she cry?"

"Because I don't remember the same good old days as she does."

Charlie ran her eye and mind back over her memories of Philip Atmor, and sighed. "What guys like you know about women could be written with a broadbrush pen on the head of a pin," she advised him. "That bell means that visiting hours are over."

"Ah, I forgot." He stood up beside the bed. "I keep forgetting that you're a woman with lots of experience. What do you hear from James?"

"Not a word," she replied. The conversation had taken a strange turn, one that she didn't care for at all. James? When it came back to her, her face turned blush red. Which Phil didn't help.

"You've got to leave," the nurse who came into the room announced. "You should have gone ten minutes ago."

"Yeah," Phil agreed as he leaned over the bed and kissed Charlie handsomely. "For luck," he added.

"I don't need a lot more luck," she whispered. "Lately it's turned out to be all bad."

"I said you have to get out now," the nurse added with more enthusiasm than common sense.

"Not luck for you," he told Charlie. "For me. I'm the one who needs the luck if I'm going to play in this league. Maybe I need more than just one kiss to do it." And he came back around the bed and tried his luck again. I don't know if that sigh means it was good or bad, Charlie thought. It certainly was expressive.

"I know," Phil told the nurse as he held up his hand. "I'm going. I'm going!" And he stalked off into the corridor and out into the night, leaving Charlie more puzzled than ever about *his* intentions and *her* feelings.

"Lovely looking man," her nurse said as she came over to adjust pillows and take readings and fill out charts.

"Yes, lovely," Charlie agreed when the thermometer was pulled out from under her tongue. "But I wish I knew what the devil he's talking about!"

CHAPTER EIGHT

PHIL came for Charlie just before noon, after an hour of arguments with the administration and the billing department. "I didn't mean for you to pay the bills," she said as he helped her out of the wheelchair. She fumbled with her crutches. "I have medical insurance."

"I don't see why I shouldn't, love. I'm the one who caused the damage." Love? What a—lovely thought, she told herself as she shifted clumsily into the front seat. Despite his many faults, there's a speck of warmth and good in the man. I ought to try to keep him. But Emily has the same idea, and she's years ahead of me.

She leaned back in her seat, but her thinking process was violently disturbed. Sam was in the back. He squealed a welcome, and managed to balance himself so his hind legs were on the back seat, and his forelegs on the back of her seat. His cool sweet muzzle was close enough to kiss. Or lick, rather, which Sam proceeded to do with great enthusiasm. Charlie scratched behind his ears.

"He acts as if nobody loves him any more," she admonished Phil. Then she turned back to Sam and crooned, "Someone loves you, boy. Namely me. Love every inch of you!'' Sam was so enthused that his hindquarters wiggled north while his forequarters wiggled south. As a result his legs slipped off the back seat, and he collapsed between the seats, and decided to stay there.

"And that reminds me,'' she said. "How's my bird? Have you been feeding him and—?''

"I have,'' he interrupted her. "I swear on my mother's grave I've been keeping him warm and feed—''

"Your mother is still alive,'' she said sternly. "How can I trust you when you tell me lies all the time?''

"Not lies,'' he maintained. "A little fanciful stuff, I confess, but not outright lies. I am a good-hearted, lovable fellow.''

"So you say,'' she muttered. "Is everything else going well?''

"Yes, but we do have this small problem,'' Phil said as he started the engine and moved out into the traffic. "For some reason I can't fathom, Emily hates Sam. Or fears him. Or something. Almost impossible to believe, isn't it?''

"Almost impossible,'' Charlie answered. "Why don't you suggest to Miss Emily that she hit the road?''

"What, right out in the open like that?'' He shook his head, afforded her one quick glance, and paid attention to his driving.

"Right out in the open,'' Charlie muttered under her breath. "Zingo, like the guillotine!''

"What?''

"Nothing at all. Nothing." Right at that moment a thought had struck her. If he won't *send* her away, why don't I *chase* her away? Yes, it would take a considerable amount of—scheming. Well, all right, a lot of lying, but don't they say "All's fair in love and war"? Well, this is war, Emily Freitas! And then Phil punctured her balloon.

"Emily's an old family friend," he commented. Charlie's eyes were on the scenery passing by, and so she missed the look he flashed at her, examining, testing, probing. "I'm not sure what I'd like in her case. Did you know that we were so close to being married that it wasn't even funny?"

That certainly got Charlie's attention; she whirled around and glared at him, missing once again the scheming smile that tugged at the sides of his mouth and as quickly disappeared. If it hadn't been for the crutches she might have told him to stop right there so she could get out and walk the rest of the way. But she hadn't the nerve. If she had yelled at him it would have reduced her own anger. Charlie knew she hadn't the nerve, and blamed it all on her hospital stay.

No, she told herself, I'll tell him to slow down enough so I can reach the darned crutches stuffed in the back seat. Then I'll bash him over the head with them! His coming *that* close to the cliffs of matrimony with Emily Freitas didn't sound the least bit funny!

Charlie stretched and took a deep breath of the salt-laden air. Now that she was committed to a course of action she could relax. I've never tasted anything so refreshing as the iodine smell of the sea, she told herself. A pair of fluffy white clouds raced across the blue sky, outdistancing the gulls. Out in the inner harbor she saw a plume of pure white climb skyward from a working tugboat. Moments later her ears were assaulted by the whistle that caused the plume.

The noise broke up her reverie as she reconsidered her problem. The eternal triangle, she told herself. I may not be heavily armed in this war, but I'm going to fight for him nonetheless. And through all this Phil Atmor kept his eyes on the road and a tuneless whistle on his lips, as if he had no idea in the world of what she was thinking.

When his Porsche rumbled over the planks of the floating bridge something caught her eye. "Is the bridge too low or the tide too high?"

"Maybe both," he answered noncommittally. "We'll be at the spring tide in a few days, and a full moon at the same time."

"And what's that mean?" she demanded to know. "Getting answers from you down-east Yankees is like pulling teeth from a bull with your bare hands."

"You've got that wrong," he chided her. "Down-east Yankees are shore folk who live *north* of Boston. Where the devil were you raised?"

"Not where you think," she grumbled at him. And then—because he stared at her as if demanding an answer, or else—she added, "Salem."

"Good Lord, I should have checked that out weeks ago," he teased. "Were there any witches in *your* family?"

"Cut that out," she yelled at him, and then, realizing he was only trying to get at her, she dropped back into her seat and continued to stare at the scenery until they came up into the driveway, and there was Beth Southerland, standing at the side door, dabbing at her eyes with a handkerchief.

"Well now, lass," the housekeeper said as she came around the house. "That good it is to see you." Beth opened the door; Sam instantly crowded by her and headed for his little swimming pool. "Pigs," Beth snorted as she hugged Charlie to her capacious bosom. "Although I ain't saying he's not a lovable comfort when there's nobody else around. Swing your feet out, while I put the crutches under your arms. Does it hurt?"

Charlie managed to balance herself on the crutches, feeling the lurch as the rubber-tipped shafts slipped in the sandy soil. "Not a bit," she replied. "Nothing broken—"

"This time," the housekeeper interrupted. Charlie felt as if someone had suddenly hit her over the head with a club. A blaze of light followed. There was the campaign, right in front of her eyes!

"Where's Emily?" Phil asked.

"She came downstairs at ten o'clock," Beth replied. "And when I told her you couldn't possibly be back before two o'clock she said something about going back to bed, and would I please call her when you came. Something like that. I've fixed you some lunch."

"I'm not hungry," he said. "Want me to carry you, Charlie?"

"I'm starving," she said at almost the same moment as he. "No, I think I can get along all right."

Sam, having soaked himself in the cool water, came trotting back. Directly to Charlie he came, and came up on to his hind legs, knocking her loose from one of the crutches.

"Oh, Lord," Charlie moaned. "Not again." It wasn't the loss of the crutch she was mourning. As she started to fall to one side Phil caught her gently and lifted her up off the ground. Once more she was back in his arms, turned so her firm full breasts were flattened against his chest. And here I thought I had overcome that little—failing, she thought. But, if I can't keep my distance, how can I survive?

"All very nice," he murmured in her ear, and then, while Beth Southerland had her back turned and was corralling Sam, Phil nibbled on her earlobe. She struggled for—oh, twenty seconds, before giving up the debate and relaxing against his warmth. "You—you low-down viper," she whispered at him, but her heart wasn't in it. "I hope you break a tooth on my earrings."

"A pro forma protest," he judged, and squeezed her gently. "Isn't it?" The pressure increased just the slightest.

"I can't breathe," she protested. He added just a touch more pressure. "Yes, damn you," she said, sighing. "Yes. Don't squeeze me to death, Philip Atmor!"

"Oh, dear, where's Philip?"

Charlie looked over her shoulder. The blond bombshell was standing on the lowest step of the stairs in what was supposed to be a seductive pose. She was dressed in a delightful Japanese kimono, a black robe with yellow dragons on each side, and a flash of golden flame spurting from each dragon's mouth. Emily looked a beauty, and Charlie, who was unfortunately born with the need to say nice things, told her so.

"Oh, this? It's just something I threw on for lounging. My father brought it back from Tokyo just for me. Isn't it lovely?"

"Lovely," Charlie agreed again. She knew the robe wasn't all that good. It reminded her of the junk one could buy in Japan on any street corner. And Charlie was accustomed to judging such things. She had played five concerts in two years in Tokyo, Nagoya, and Osaka.

"And Philip is—?"

"Had to go into town," Charlie reported. "Miss Sylvia called with something rather urgent."

Emily, having posed long enough for her purposes, came down the stairs and took the rocking chair. Charlie was sitting in the window seat with her violin before her. "A bossy woman," Emily said as she rocked a time or two. "When I take over this house—" this man, Charlie thought, not this house "—I'm going to see some changes made. And one of them is that Claudia Sylvia has got to go!"

"Shhhush." Charlie set a cautionary finger across her own lips. "If Mrs. Southerland hears..." she whispered. "You *do* know that the pair of them are cousins?"

Emily, caught up in the conspiracy, blushed and looked around hastily. "You mean Mrs. Southerland and Claudia?"

"The very pair," Charlie whispered. "They talk. Word gets around. And you know how Philip is."

"I don't believe any of this that you're telling me," Emily said, but there was a little quaver in her voice. "I've known Philip for almost all my life. He would never do anything to—"

"You're probably right," Charlie interrupted. "As an old family friend and all that. Of course, before I moved in with him he was as sweet as can be. That was my mistake. Living with him. But—" she let the word hang in the air as she nibbled at her lower lip "—but I'm certain that he's changed, Emily. Thirteen years, is it? Thirteen years ago that you dumped him? You don't think he might hold that against you?"

Emily Freitas was a woman no longer sure of herself. "You lived with him? What are you saying?" she whispered.

Charlie held up her right hand, still in its embryonic cast. "Look, I don't want to scare you," she said solemnly. "Yes, I've been living with that man for almost nine months. I had no past history of hatred with Philip. I thought we were getting along fine. And then one afternoon I said something about Miss Sylvia. Nothing terribly important, you understand. Well, before I could get my mouth closed he swung on me, knocked me across the room, and then came over and glared at me. No explanation—not a word given. And then he . . ." One manufactured tear, Charlie told herself. This story is so morbid that I almost believe it myself! The tear came.

"And then what happened?" Emily was bending as close to the window seat as she could get, her eyes wide as fifty-cent pieces, and a little shiver working at the dimple on her left cheek.

Charlie made one more attempt to add a second tear, but had to give it up. A thespian she was not, but she had read many a Gothic tale to the younger girls during her last year in the orphanage, and her voice met the requirement now.

"He—he cursed something terrible," she muttered. "Like some mad sailor, you know." Her audience of one nodded her head and shivered again. "And then he said," Charlie continued, dragging it out for all it was worth, "he said, 'I'm going to teach you a lesson.' And then he stepped on my hand. Would you believe that, Emily? Stepped on my bow hand and broke my finger! Would you believe it?"

Emily would. She jumped to her feet, holding the back of one shaking hand to her mouth, sobbed in desperation, and ran for the stairs. Where she promptly fell over Sam, scrambled to her feet again, and dashed up the stairs.

"Charlotte MacEnnaly," Mrs. Southerland said from the safety of the kitchen door, "what a terrible lie! Terrible!"

"Oh, did you really think so, Beth?" Charlie shifted around to pick up her violin. The bow had been tightened and the strings tuned. She tucked the instrument under her chin and ran a quick scale in D flat. "I thought it was rather good, myself. All the right touches.''

''You may be right,'' the housekeeper said as she dabbed her apron to her eyes and wiped away the tears of laughter. ''You may be right, but what if the mister... ?''

Charlie felt the shock wave. If the mister finds out—and doesn't appreciate the effort? Doesn't understand that I'm doing it all for him? As he won't! Oh, Lord! She put her instrument back in place and spent a bone-wearying thirty minutes doing the scales.

Two weeks later Charlie was idly playing her violin from memory when Phil walked into the living room, which she had taken over for her music room.

''That's beautiful,'' he said in some awe. It was the first time he had paid any real attention to her playing. ''What is it?''

''Oh, just a medley of this and that,'' she told him, grinning at him. ''The first piece was a selection from *Sheherezade*. The second was part of Smetana's *Die Moldau*.''

''And the third?''

''A real American tone poem, Philip. That's the first movement of Ferde Grofé's *Grand Canyon Suite*. What do you think?''

''I'm not sure,'' he said, and she could see the wicked gleam in his eye. ''The bowing is a little choppy, I believe.''

''Darn you, Phil Atmor!'' She rose to the bait like a hungry trout in the town stream. ''Three weeks ago you didn't even know which hand you hold the bow in, and now you're a critic!''

"I learn fast," he boasted, and ducked as she picked up a pillow and hurled it at him. "Now wait a darn minute," he protested as he stood up, with both hands elevated in a surrender mode. "I've got other things to think about with you declaring war on me. Sit down here for a minute—please."

It was the "please" that did her in. She couldn't ever remember him saying the word before. Charlie gently put her violin back into its temporary case and sank onto the couch, patting the space next to her with one hand.

"I do believe your hand is improving," he said. "Are you comfortable in my house?"

"How could I not be? You tore up your dining room to provide me with a downstairs bedroom. You surrender your living room every morning for my music practice, and you're—just ever so nice about everything. I keep one eye turned over my shoulder, for fear the real you is tailing me!"

"The real me? Here's the real me," he said as he moved over on the couch, wrapped two huge arms around her, and planted a kiss on her nose. "Let that be a lesson to you!"

"Oh, it will, it will. I always learn from my mistakes—maybe I'm a little slow, but I learn. Now, how was that again?" He tried to repeat the instruction, but her little button nose wiggled out of the way and he landed full on her warm lips. At first she let him lead, then, as the fervor struck, she reached both hands up around his neck and refused to let him move away.

"Was that it?" she asked breathlessly a few moments later.

"Yeah, well, I think you're getting better at it," he said, chuckling.

"We could try again if you insist, Phil." Just at that moment Emily came sauntering down the stairs.

"What is it you're trying?" the blonde asked. "Something we can all play?"

"No, I don't think so," Charlie said. "Phil was teaching me something about music. At least I *think* that's what he was doing. Mrs. Southerland had to go into town to do some shopping. She left you some breakfast in the kitchen."

"Well, now that I've got you all organized, I think I have to go to work," Phil said. "You ladies have a good time. I'm pleased to see how well you are all getting along. Anything I can bring you home?"

"Some magazines," Emily managed to squeeze in. "Something more sophisticated than the *Seafarer's Annual*, or that *Guide to Navigation*."

"Sure," he agreed. "I know just the person to help me make a selection. And you, Charlie?"

"Now that you bring it to mind," Charlotte said, "I'd like a hammer, a tube of caulking compound, and some ten-penny nails."

"Planning to build us a new bridge?" Phil asked.

"Not me. I'm planning to build an ark," Charlie commented. "But yes, we need a new bridge, don't we? That old thing has—"

"Has been there for nigh on to fifty years," Phil interrupted, "and the selectmen seem to feel it could go another fifty, they tell me. Put your mind to something more possible. Farewell, my lovelies—parting is such sweet sorrow."

"Harvard," Charlie muttered disgustedly under her breath. "Can't even quote Shakespeare properly."

"Yes, isn't it?" Emily trilled as she rushed across the room and threw herself at Phil. I've got to remember that act, Charlie thought. She's getting a grade "A" kiss, and I don't think I care for that! Especially since Phil looks as if he enjoyed the hell out of it. Shape up, Miss Emily Freitas, or ship out! Get your claws off my man. And just to make a point— well, I will in a minute. Make a point, that is, as soon as Phil is out of sight and hearing. And in the meantime she gave him a class-four glare, and muttered a very cold, "G'bye" as he walked out of the door, whistling. And then, as a flush-faced Emily strolled out into the kitchen, apparently lost in daydreams, Charlie picked up her violin and went back to basic fingering and bowing practices, over and over and over.

"It's been almost two hours," Emily complained as she came wandering back out of the kitchen. "Can't you stop that wailing?"

Charlie, who was playing as poorly as was possible without her violin snapping a string at her, lowered her bow and shook her head.

"Do you play an instrument, Emily?" she asked mildly.

"Of course. Piano and accordion," the blonde replied. "My family has always been very culture oriented."

"Yes, I thought you might be." Charlie flexed her fingers for a time. After a six-week layoff, her muscles were considerably out of tone. "If I could give you some advice, Emily?"

"Why would you want to give me any advice?" Emily snapped. "We're not boon companions, after all. You're on your way out, and I'm on my way in, only this time I mean to get his ring on my finger before I—"

"Yes," Charlie interrupted, "I understand. But we're still two women, Emily, living in a man's world. I wouldn't want you to go through the things I've experienced."

"Such as?"

"Don't ever tell him that you can play anything," Charlie whispered.

"Oh? So you can hold the center stage in music around here?"

"Me?" Charlie broke up into laughter, a bitter laughter. "Believe me, if I had it all to do over again I would never have mentioned music to Philip."

"So tell me," the blonde said.

"Well, of course you know that Phil is tone deaf. Completely tone deaf. I'm sure you heard him whistling when he went out. He thinks that's music. And the only sort of music he'll put up with is country."

"And if he doesn't get it?"

"He can't tell one song from another, but he's a typical New Englander. He's willing to believe the worst about anyone at the drop of a hat. What did you think happened to my leg?''

"You mean—?"

"Yup. I was playing Rimsky-Korsakov, and he claimed I was mocking him, and he—"

"Good Lord, he beat you up again?"

"Not exactly," Charlie said. It is hard to lie through your teeth, she told herself. I don't know whether to spread it on thicker, or get out while I'm able. "No, he didn't exactly beat me up. He just kicked me on my knee and knocked me across the room!"

"I don't believe that," Emily muttered. "I—why are you telling me all this?"

"I told you before. I'm leaving in a little while, Emily, and I'd feel guilty about it if I didn't tell you everything that I know about Phil. We women have a hard enough time without having to put up with a bully." And now a tear or two, she told herself, but with no good result. So she turned away from the other woman, picked up her instrument, and started for her bedroom. "Well, don't pay me any attention, dear," she said. "You're bigger than I am, and I suppose you know what you're doing with men like Phil. But—do be careful!" And on that high note she made her exit before she spoiled the whole act.

The next morning was clear and sultry, the result of a Bermuda high weather system, and when Charlie broke the news to Phil both the weather and the conversation grew unbearable.

"So why, after all this time, do you have to move back into your own house?" he demanded. He was glaring at her so hard that his spoon missed the round trip between cereal and mouth, and he ended up with milk dripping down off his chin.

"Don't yell at me at the breakfast table! In fact, don't yell at me at all." She pushed back her bowl, ready to play hardball across the table. "I don't have to get your permission to take myself back to my own house, you know." All of which had the makings of a grand and glorious fight—but Phil withdrew almost immediately, a totally uncharacteristic move on his part. There was a moment of silence, in which only Beth Southerland made soft noises around the kitchen stove.

"Well, if you can't stand the heat I suppose you'd best get out of the kitchen," Phil finally said. I didn't exactly mean today, Charlie thought to herself as she rescued her bowl and industriously worked on her own cereal. You could have played the game for a little while longer. But no, everything is flat down and go, huh?

"Well?" Phil asked.

"Well indeed," Charlie responded, and then clamped her lips shut as she struggled back up to her feet. Her hand had made considerable progress; in fact, she expected the doctor would take off the cast this same afternoon. As for her knee, the swelling had gone down far enough to make moving on crutches endurable. And, on top of that, the veterinarian had given her the release order for her gull. "And so I'm going," she told him as she pushed her way out of the kitchen.

"Have a good life," he commented. He couldn't even get up from the table, Charlie told herself. What sort of a relationship is this? He bangs me around and gives me a hard time, and in between times he wants me to kiss him! It wouldn't be so much of a problem if I didn't find the kissing part so darned enjoyable. So she marched off to her bedroom, and then tried to figure out how she was going to move. The answer was just behind her. Beth Southerland had followed her.

"It's good of you to help," Charlie acknowledged. "I don't understand how a nice woman like you can exist with such a..."

She could not quite find the word. "Nasty," Beth suggested.

"Yeah, that'll do very well. Nasty man." She savored the word for a moment. Just quite correct. A nasty man. Except for—except for nothing, Charlotte MacEnnaly. Except for nothing. "Beth, if you would pack my bag, I could be out in the yard turning Hank loose."

"Hank?"

"My gull. Today is the day, the vet said, to turn him loose."

"It would be better, love, if *I* were to drag that big cage out into the yard, and *you* pack the clothes."

Charlie's good humor was back. "You don't know how very much I hate to pack clothes. Why don't we—?"

"Both go out and release the darn bird?" the housekeeper interrupted. And so they did. When the lid of his cage was lifted, the gull seemed to shrink back into a corner for a moment. Then, after his jet black eyes confirmed that both the women were at some distance, he gave a staggering leap, fluttered his wings gently, and then was gone, climbing like a passenger jet into the eye of the sun. Charlie watched him, with one hand up as a sunshade. The gull climbed to some height, then circled above them, diving to inspect his former prison until his own life sphere called him.

"Do you think he'll come back?" Charlie asked, sounding somewhat sad.

"I doubt it," Beth replied. "That's why they call things birdbrained."

"It—I just hate coming to endings," Charlie commented. "I wonder what we ought to do about the cage. The darn thing is heavy."

"Leave it until the mister comes home," Beth told her. "Men have their uses. Now, about the suitcases?"

"What's going on here?" Emily was down, earlier than usual. *Much* earlier than usual.

"Your favorite day has come," Charlie announced, laughing. "I'm leaving. Going home!"

"That *is* something," Emily said, and then surprised the others completely. "Leaving? It couldn't happen to a nicer girl. Let me help you pack!"

The only member of the family who failed to find joy in it all was Sam. As Charlie came out of the house, leading the parade, he sat down in front of her and gave a crying little squeal. "But I have to go, Sam," she told him. It's part of the scheme of things." When she hobbled around him he turned and followed, complaining all the way.

By noon the move was complete; Beth had offered her a motherly hug, Emily had cockily tipped a finger salute, and Sam had been shooed off. Charlie was tired. She made herself a cup of tea, scrounged a couple of crackers from the old box that had stood on her shelf for weeks, then wiggled her way into a wraparound blue skirt and a demure lace blouse—a casual look around the house—and she went out the door. Sam, of course, was sitting on the porch. He got up and followed her to her car.

"No, Sam. Go home."

He acted like an animal whose ears had betrayed him. "Go home," she commanded, and then ducked around to the driver's side of the car and slipped into the seat. Sam, moving slower than was usually his wont, watched the door slam and separate them. Then he stalked over to the side of the road and mourned.

The nurse looked at Charlie's appointment card. "You're late," she accused. "The doctor's time is valuable."

"I'm fifteen minutes early," Charlie said very firmly. Doctors and lawyers, she told herself as she sat in the waiting room twenty-five minutes later. We ought to treat them the way the old Romans did— make them municipal slaves. But it wasn't all that terrible a day. The doctor finally came whistling by her only fifty minutes after her appointment time. He checked her hand, mumbling as he did so. Three minutes' worth. And then he checked her knee, still mumbling. Four minutes. After which he said something to Charlie in the medical language, and disappeared.

"That cast comes off now," the nurse interpreted. "The knee looks pretty good, but you're standing on it too much. Come back in two weeks.'' After which Charlie found herself ushered into an examination room, the cast did come off, and the *bill* was already prepared by the time she reached the front door. But, when the clerk discovered that Charlie had medical insurance, which would pay the bills, she smiled, and was willing to spare a word or two in casual conversation.

The supermarket was something else. Charlie was known to the manager, a young man of twenty-four, who had a great affection for famous women with nice figures. He found an assistant to push Charlie's cart and empty the gear into her car. The manager himself came to the door to see her off.

"We must go dancing some time, Miss Mac-Ennaly," he suggested. Charlie looked down at her crutches and shrugged her shoulders. And then drove back to the island.

"And how's the campaign going?" Claudia Sylvia walked around the room, checking her flowers just before home time, her normal procedure.

"Not too well," Phil said as he leaned back and put his feet up on his desk. "I think I may have overdone things this morning. But when she talked about moving out I figured I'd really blown the works. I don't know why I worry about things like that. After all, she's only a redheaded fiddle player. Oops! Violinist."

"What do you mean, overdone things?" Claudia reached for her watering pot. Not that the cactus needed water, but she dared not turn her face so that Phil could see the laughter in her eyes.

"Oh, it was something I read in a magazine. A guy has this girl, see, and she's not too keen on him, so he plays hot and cold alternately until he gets her confused, then whammy, he moves in on her! You see?"

"Oh, yes, I see," Claudia replied. "Of course. Whammy. That is, if you're sure which one of you is thoroughly confused. Hot and cold?"

"Yeah. Only this morning I think it got too cold. I thought having Emily around would provoke a little jealousy."

"And it didn't?"

"You know," he mused, "courting a woman is like being the sorcerer's apprentice. You have to be extra careful of your potions and magic. Here I've worked hard for more than a couple of weeks. Emily's jealous as hell and Charlie's acting as if she were a bystander!"

"I wonder where you got all this information," Claudia said. "Six months ago if you were chasing a girl you would have needed a 'how-to-do-it' manual."

"That's not really true," he protested. "Oh, I've asked around. Unfortunately I don't seem to get the same answer from any of the dozen people I've talked to."

"That's probably why you don't see a great many married fishermen."

"Yeah, well. I think I'd better get going."

"Yes, you do that," Claudia agreed. And then, moments after she saw his car come up the drive from the underground parking lot, "Maybe I'd better have a word with this girl," she told the flowers. "She doesn't have a mother of her own. Phil's a philanderer of the first water. Charlie seems to be lost. Wouldn't it be one hell of a wedding night, to find out that neither one of them knows what they're supposed to do?" Even the roses blushed.

Phil drove out into the sunshine, reminding himself that he had always wanted a convertible. Traffic was building up. June was a day short of completion. The schools were out and the beaches were loaded. Which is a good time, he reminded himself, to have his oil tanks filled. During the slack summer season the price of heating oil dropped considerably. As he turned off route six, heading down the Neck, he called his oil company through his car telephone, and placed the order.

The old homestead is peaceful, he assured himself as he zoomed up the drive. Sam came to meet him as he got out. "Something wrong, old boy?" His pet pig seemed to be drooping. When Phil scratched him behind the ears the mini-pig managed to take one lick at his hand, and then he wandered off. Sickening for something, Phil told himself as he went into the house.

Beth Southerland was sitting at the kitchen table, having a cup of tea. Normally she rose when the mister came in. Today she rested her chin between her hands, and sighed.

"I can see there's a funeral," he said, "but I don't know who's dead."

"All of us," Beth murmured. "Emily's still here, and Charlie's gone."

"Well, don't worry about that," he said. "We'll reverse the process soon enough. What time is Charlie coming back?"

"As far as I can guess, never."

"Never?" His stomach began to roil. "Never?"

"She took all her belongings with her," Beth replied. "Set her gull free, took all her worldly goods, and went home. Then after a while I saw her come back, unload something, and drive off down the south road."

"Not back to the bridge road?"

"No, just down the dirt road that runs around the island."

Guilty, his conscience roared at him. You pressed the little game too far, you idiot. Now what?

"Have some soup," Beth pressed him, setting a bowl in front of him.

Automatically his hand picked up a spoon and began to scoop. The soup tasted like nothing. "You'd better wait until I put something in the bowl," Beth chided him. "You seem to be bothered as much as Charlie was after she had that talk with Emily."

"Charlie talked with Emily?" It was the key word that brought him back to reality. "Talked with Emily?"

Beth nodded. Phil pushed back from the table and walked purposefully out into the living room. *"Emily!"* he roared up the stairs. There was a scrambling noise from the room at the head of the stairs.

"Phil? You're not really angry with me are you? Phil?"

"I'll show you angry," he muttered. "Come down here and tell me what you said to Charlie today."

"You—about Charlie? Honestly, I can't play at all, Philip. Not a note!"

"I don't care if you can't play a penny whistle," he roared. "I want to know what you said to Charlie this morning!"

"I—didn't say anything to her," Emily squeaked. "She said—"

"What did she say?"

"Please don't roar at me, Philip. She said—she was leaving and I—"

"Damn it, woman, stop sniffling! Come on down here."

Emily evidently found some spare store of courage. "I will *not*," she yelled at him. "You're not going to treat *me* like that!"

"I'm not going to treat you like what?" He was trying to be gentle, but his upstairs audience began sobbing, dashed back into her room, slammed the door behind her, and locked it.

"Still having trouble?" Beth, behind him in the kitchen doorway, was slipping into her light sweater, preparing to leave for home.

"You wouldn't believe," he sighed. "Look, I don't see your in-laws' car. How are you going to get home?"

"I don't know," the housekeeper replied. "Ellie should have been here a half hour ago. I don't know what—"

"Tell you what," he announced. "Since nobody else is speaking to me today, suppose I run you home?"

"That would be nice, Mr. Atmor. If you could take me to the bus stop?"

"Nonsense," he said as he helped her into the Porsche. "All the way, Ms. Beth. That's the way it is. You're my only real love."

"Go on with you," the housekeeper said, and blushed. Let that teach you a sharp lesson, he told himself as he started the engine. Our Ms. Beth must be all of sixty-five, and still she can blush. He was still shaking his head when he turned out into the road and around the slight curve that led to the floating bridge.

"Oh, my goodness," Phil Atmor said as he slammed on the brakes.

"Dear me," Beth Southerland said as she clutched shamelessly at his shoulder.

Emily Freitas peeped out of the window of her second-floor bedroom, and watched as the Porsche started down the driveway. She was still trembling at her narrow escape. But he certainly wouldn't be gone long, and when he came back she would be alone with him. And that was something she could not stand.

"Thank the Lord for Charlie MacEnnaly," she muttered as she fumbled for the most important of all her possessions, and shoved them into a plain plastic bag. She knew that, but for herself, the house was empty. She came down the stairs like a thief in the night, and stole out of the side door, being careful not to let it slam.

Whatever she had to do, she must not go to the bridge. He might be returning at any moment, and see her. *That* trip must be later, after he had returned. For now she would have to duck out of sight—maybe beg shelter in Charlie's house?

In the end there was no need for begging. Charlotte MacEnnaly's house stood open and empty, but guarded by Sam, who was stretched out on the MacEnnaly porch, guarding. For ten minutes Emily tried to persuade—from a safe distance—the mini-pig away from the door. But, when the Porsche came back up to the house, Sam decamped to welcome his master. Emily sneaked quietly into the house, locked the door behind her, and collapsed in a chair, shaking with fear.

CHAPTER NINE

CHARLIE began to regret her little expedition at about four o'clock in the afternoon. It had taken her more than an hour to pull and tug the flat-bottomed row boat up on the beach, and another hour to caulk all the seams. It all seemed so easy in the guidebook from the hardware store, but that book, of course, hadn't included a laborer on crutches, with one hand barely released into the sunshine.

And now, she told herself, all I have to do is nail the darn pier back together. Right after I eat one of these sandwiches. So she stretched herself out on the sand and went about the feeding business. And that, as usual, was the time for Sam to track her down. "Poor boy," she comforted him. "You're fading away to a tub of lard. Doesn't anybody feed you these days?"

Sam grumbled an honest agreement, and settled down to share a sandwich. Not the homemade kind; that was still beyond Charlie's culinary skill. But Sam was definitely a member of the proletariat. He ate anything, with anybody, at any time.

"And where is Captain Philip Bluebeard?" she asked. Sam looked up at her and gave a noncommittal grunt before he went nosing through the empty paper bags. "All gone, boy," she confessed. "I'm dieting."

Sam knew *that* word. He gave her an outraged squeal and withdrew into the shade under the pier. "And the same to you," she called after him in her most cheerful voice.

Charlie looked at the boat again. She had pushed it off the sand for a few feet, and it looked as if it might be floating. But, since she knew as much about boats as she did about Japanese dragons, she felt handicapped. She knew that there were supposed to be two oars, and she had only one.

"But what the hey," she called down to Sam. "It's really not a yacht—it's just busy work. You understand?"

Sam was still holding on to the hurt of the word "diet," and refused an answer. "So I'll talk to myself," she announced proudly. "Do you know the old song about the lady who walked down the sidewalk, and there in the gutter were a man and a pig, fast asleep? So she sang,

"You can tell a man who boozes
By the company he chooses.
And the pig got up and slowly walked away!"

It was too much for Sam. He glared up at her, grumbled as mean a reply as a pig might speak, and slowly walked away.

Charlie shook her head, not knowing whether or not it was the words or her singing to which Sam objected. But there was still some sun left in the day. She picked up her hammer and began to reinforce the rickety old pier.

Sunset, on a New England summer day, came around at about seven-thirty. But at five the sun was already setting in the west, color laden by the polluted air that was locked in over Fairhaven, the harbor, and New Bedford. The only gulls airborne were the flock following two fishing boats into the harbor, dumping their rubbish astern as they came. It was all illegal, but the birds were fast losing their ability to fish because man and his rubbish met all their requirements without the expenditure of much effort.

Still, pollution or no, there was always some arcane beauty to somebody else's rubbish, and a sun diving into the soot. Charlie pulled her legs up under her in as much of a yoga position as her knee would allow, and wallowed unashamedly in the schmaltz of it all. If it hadn't been for Sam squealing at her she might never have heard the new arrival. Charlie turned to look over her shoulder.

"Emily? You look like somebody who's been dragged backward through a hedge. What's wrong?"

There was just enough sympathy in her voice to turn on the watering pot. Emily, standing at the near end of the pier, began to run in Charlie's direction, and the tears ran like a monsoon rain. Charlie struggled to her feet just in time to receive the sobbing woman.

"I should have listened to you," Emily blurted out after she had had her cry. "I didn't believe at all, but he was mad, and cursing, and I thought he was going to beat me right there on the spot! Lord, what a rotten man."

Well there's something I could agree on, Charlie thought. In spades. He was indeed a rotten man, but that really wasn't what Emily wanted to hear. "Now, now. I'm sure he didn't mean exactly what you thought he said. Perhaps you misunderstood?"

"Oh, he meant it all right. Every darn word. I told him I couldn't play a note, and he roared at me—something about playing a penny flute. Or maybe he said I could do—something with the penny flute. I don't quite know exactly what he said, but it was very nasty. I wouldn't do anything like that. Not ever. And how could you play a penny flute if you—? Lord, what a vile man!"

"So, maybe you're entirely right," Charlie said, sighing. "The wolf has turned into the wolf, right?"

"Right." The blonde squatted down on the ancient planks and searched the horizon. "I've got to get off this island!"

"The bridge is back in the other direction," Charlie offered. "About a quarter of a mile, I'd guess. Why don't you just—?"

"I can't," Emily interrupted. She was back in her rain mode. Surely, Charlie thought, there'll be a massive high tide tonight if she doesn't stop crying?

Emily stood up. All her sophistication had disappeared. Her thin cotton dress had been ripped at the bodice. Dirt smeared her usually immaculate throat, and her long blond hair straggled. "I waited—in your house—till he came back from the bridge and went into his house." A questioning pause.

"I don't mind," Charlie said. "Any old port in a storm. And then what did you do?"

"And then I sneaked out in a big circle around both houses and walked down to the bridge. Oh, Lord!" More tears. Not as many as before. Her eyes must be getting pretty dry by now, Charlie thought.

Emily took a grip on herself, shuddered, and settled down, speaking quickly. "And the bridge is out of service," she half whispered. "One of those big oil trucks tried to cross over, and the wheels went through the planking. What's left of the bridge is underwater. There are a couple of fire trucks at the scene, and a tow truck, but I wasn't going to try to cross over on just those beams. Not me."

"Wow! And I thought *I* was leading a fast life," Charlie said. "All you need is a hurricane, and we'd have a perfect plot. I envy you."

"Hurricane. There's a hurricane coming? I've got to get off this island," the other woman cried. "With all that, and him too? Do you suppose he might come and track me down?"

"I doubt it," Charlie replied. "Sam's the only tracker on the island, and he's playing best out of sight under the pier." Emily hugged herself with both arms and peered over the side of the pier.

"I knew there was something wrong with that man. Even back when we were first engaged, there was something about him that didn't quite fit. A grown man, mind you, and a pet pig? Whoever heard of such a thing?"

"Whoever did?" Charlie murmured agreement. To her, Philip and his pet pig had become *very* acceptable, in fact, even lovable. But you didn't say something like that to a woman you were trying to get rid of!

"That boat," Emily asked. "Does it float?"

"I'm not sure," Charlie mused. "Do you swim?"

"Some."

"I think the boat might float some," Charlie reported. Even panic-stricken Emily could hear the doubt in her voice. "Well, I've never caulked a boat before," Charlie added, aggrieved. "I did the best I could. But I didn't actually test it out. I can't swim a stroke."

The blonde looked her over suspiciously. Poor Emily might have been born of ten seafaring generations, for all Charlie knew. "There's only one oar," the blonde said.

"That's right," Charlie responded. "I don't know how you make a row boat go—with one oar or two. Maybe you'd better not try it."

The decision hung in the balance. Emily definitely wanted to go, and only fear held her back. Starting from the pier, the island was about a hundred yards from the mainland—a good football field's length—and the little wavelets were beginning to beat up a froth.

Then Sam heard something, squealed loudly enough to herald the second coming, and dashed off up the beach. "He's almost here," Charlie announced dolefully.

"He?"

"Philip Atmor. That's their private code, you know."

"Pigs can't talk," Emily said stoutly. "That's pure nonsense!"

"Ah, but Sam is descended from a long line of miniature Vietnamese pigs," Charlie said.

A yell from behind them, in a deep male voice. "Emily! *Emily!*"

"He's madder than a wet hen. I'm glad he's not calling for me," Charlie offered sympathetically. And that broke the logjam. Emily Freitas pulled up her skirts to thigh-level and went thundering back down the length of the pier. Charlie watched, fascinated.

The boat *was* afloat. Emily gave it another push and vaulted in over the stern. Another roar from behind them hurried her on. Or harried her? The girl picked up the single oar, sat up in the bows of the boat, and began to use it like a paddle. Charlie settled back to watch. This might be a very instructive moment. And besides, she had told the stupid woman not to go in the boat! Footsteps rattled up onto the pier behind her. The whole structure trembled. The running footsteps slacked off to a more careful approach, and then he had arrived.

"What the hell are you two crazies doing out here?" he roared.

"I'm well, and how are you, Philip?"

"Don't give me that sweet innocence," he said, at slightly less than a roar. But only slightly. "Hello, Charlie."

"Lovely sunset, Philip. See how those reds are turning blue as they mix?"

"Lovely," he snorted. "And what the hell is *she* doing?"

Charlie, who had been watching Emily's progress, shook her head. Obviously there was a great deal more about caulking a boat than she knew. Poor Emily had managed to reach the mid-point of her voyage, and there was very little dry wood left on the boat. Another half inch and water would be coming over the sides.

"Would you suppose she's trying to walk on water?"

"Don't be a—what the hell," he muttered. Charlie gave thanks; her eardrums might possibly last until morning if he just didn't roar again.

"Look at me, Charlie." He managed to get her attention by seizing her shoulders, pulling her over in front of him, and trapping her against his steel chest. "Now, watch my lips, Miss MacEnnaly. *Why* is Emily so desperately eager to get away from us?"

"I don't know all the details," Charlie said meekly, "but she seems to be under the impression that you were about to beat up on her. In fact, *she* said that *you* said that *she* could take her penny whistle and—well, that, *she* said, is something up with which she could not put!"

"And why do you suppose she had this idea that I might beat up on her?"

"Oh, I don't know, Phil. We were talking about—well, you know, you're such a big man, and I had a broken hand and a sprained knee, and I guess she was swept up in the story, perhaps. Did you know that she has the habit of embellishing simple stories?"

"You little devil," he muttered as he pushed her toward the seaward end of the pier. "*She* embellishes?"

Charlie hobbled along as best she could, having only one crutch left to support her. "There's a little bit of devil in all us women," she sighed. "I don't think she's going to make it. Her shoes are too narrow for walking on water. Hadn't you better do something?"

"Yeah, why don't *I* do something?" He was already slipping out of his shoes. When his hand moved to his belt Charlie blushed, but stayed to watch anyway. "It's always the man who gets the dirty work," he muttered as he pulled the sweater over his head. Then he stood up. By now Emily was screaming and swimming in a circle in the cold harbor water.

"That water is freezing out there," he complained. He was covered by a pair of white jockey shorts and goose pimples. The shorts left nothing at all to the imagination. He poised for a racing dive, but lacked that last smidgen of nerve. Which Sam took care of with great skill.

All the excitement had hardly taken five minutes, so far, and here came Sam, looking to be the hero. Straight out of the pier he came, his little legs moving at ten miles to the minute, his head down, reminiscent of his wild-boar ancestors of the Paleological forest. Unfortunately, this pig lacked *two* essential elements: he had no sweat glands; he also had no brakes. So, when Sam's bent head met the immovable object, Phil's posterior, the man went hurtling out to sea, coming down about fifteen feet away from the pier. And Sam, being a true pig for all seasons, blundered into Charlie, knocking her off the pier as well, and then slithered and slid until he went over the end himself, splashing around happily in the cool water.

By now Phil Atmor had exhausted his file of four-letter words, and began to stir up a fuss with his muscular Australian crawl. Emily might well have been rescued in a moment, but when her rescuer arrived on the scene he was not welcome. He finally ended the argument by coming up out of the water behind her, and clamping his left arm around her neck. Emily blustered and flustered, but, stretched out on her back, all she could do was flail at the water. Eventually she gave up the struggle; he towed the inert body over to the mainland, where he beached her like a sick whale, checked her out briefly and then abandoned her to answer the emergency call from Sam. A moment's breath was required. He knuckled at his eyes to clear his vision.

All he could see was that somebody—Charlie—was making an awful splashing, trying to reach the ladder at the end of the pier. And Sam, sweet, delightful Sam, was paddling around her like the coxswain in a four-oar boat.

It could only happen to me, Phil told himself as he knelt beside the supine Emily. Leave the woman here, unconscious, or hesitate and pray that Charlie didn't drown? Oh, hell! He looked north, along the curve of the shore. The bridge site was much closer on this side of the river than on the other. He yelled a couple of times for help. One of the uniformed figures at the bridge waved at him. He still had the debate: go for Charlie, or stay for Emily?

His dilemma was resolved by Emily. The blonde came to, stirred in the sand, looked around, and saw Phil. "Dear Lord!" she screamed as she scrambled to her feet and ran south, in the opposite direction to her possible rescuers. This time Phil's ethical debate with himself took much less time. "To hell with her," he muttered as he sprinted back into the water until it was knee-high, and made a graceful dive into the waves.

"Well, it's about time," Charlie told Phil moments later. She had reached the bottom of the ladder, urged on by several massive bumps from Sam, but hadn't the strength in hand or knee to climb. And so she clung to the rotten wood with one good hand and prayed for a miracle. And when it—or he—came close enough to make the rescue she blew her short-tempered fuse.

"I'll bet I've set a new hundred-yard record," he muttered as he came up to her and shifted her weight onto his shoulders.

"You wouldn't have to if you hadn't stopped to ogle the blonde," she snapped.

"Ogle? I haven't heard that word in years. Is it still in the dictionary?" The bottom step of the ladder, on which all their combined water weights were suspended, gave an ominous crack. He shifted his massive hand one step higher, and jiggled her weight to a better balance.

"Yes, ogle," she said. "If you would have stayed ogling for another two minutes you would have saved yourself the cost of the million-dollar lawsuit I'm going to file as soon as I get on dry land!"

"Fierce," he said, chuckling. " 'The lady doth protest too much, methinks.' "

"However in the world did you learn that? I know you went to Harvard, but I'm of the opinion that you never went into the academic building where they dispensed knowledge.'' Said with a suitable sneer, all of which gave her an additional mouthful of salt water, and left her gagging.

"Nothing I like worse than a poor loser," he returned gruffly. "C'mon, woman."

Well, at least I got that right, Phil thought as he rolled her over on her back and started to tow her to the beach. Her shorts and blouse had originally been tight enough to get a dock worker to whistle. Now, soaking wet, she looked fit enough for a gourmet meal. One of his strokes went slightly askew, landing on her neat little breast. And stuck there, as if she had layered the blouse with glue. Just stuck there. And he found it difficult to tow her along using a side stroke.

She had her lips fastened shut. Locked shut. For fear of taking another mouthful of salt water, he told himself. And that's why she hasn't said anything at all! Maybe this is the answer to our relationship. All I have to do is to barely keep her head above water.

"You can stop the pretense now," she suddenly announced. "My feet are dragging on the sand." He stopped swimming, allowing his feet to drift downward.

"Darned if you aren't right," he said. The water was actually up to his knees. "Need help getting up?"

"From you? No!"

But no amount of turning and tossing could get her feet under her. Phil knew a number of things when she spoke again. He knew that she hated to ask, that she was as bitter as a green lemon, and there was no way in the world he could get out of this problem.

"Help me," she pleaded.

He bent down and swept her up in his arms, then stood there as she dripped all over him. As she clung to him, both hands around his neck. As she nuzzled at his cheek. As she whimpered and treasured him. As he squeezed her gently and did his best to swallow her up in himself.

It was Sam who finally brought them both to their senses. Water up to Phil's knees meant being almost submerged for the little pig. He began to butt at Phil, to urge him out of the water, to squeal at him, trying to coax this huge man that he owned into doing something worthwhile. Like finding a couple more sandwiches instead of nibbling at the girl.

"Okay, okay," Phil finally acknowledged, and stepped forward a few paces until his feet told him they were on dry land. There was a warm wind blowing, but as it dried out their clothes it was chilling. For no reason he knew Phil walked with his burden to the far end of the pier and set them both down, with their feet hanging over the edge. It wasn't the answer Sam wanted, but since there was no response to his playful butts the pig gave up, circled himself a couple of times, and lay down behind them to listen.

"What the devil were you doing down here?" Phil finally asked.

"Fixing the boat," Charlie said softly. "And the pier. It seemed so easy. Just a little caulking compound and a few nails. And I was bored out of my skull just sitting at home."

"That was pretty stupid. What do you know about caulking boats? How many have you done?"

"Including this one?"

"Okay, including this one." His arm came around her shoulders, shifting her so that their thighs touched. The warmth of her soft hip sent a little quiver up his spine and his autonomic nerve system responded without command. "Well?"

"Well, including this one," she drawled languidly, "I've caulked one."

"Stupid. Absolutely stupid! Do you know you could have drowned Emily?"

She sat up straight and moved away from him. "I had that thought, but you couldn't prove it in court. Why are you picking on me?"

"And that's why you moved out of my house!" It was a cast in the dark, but it struck full in the target circle.

"Did you think I was going to stand around while you played house with that blonde—?"

"I'll be damned!" he exclaimed. "Jealousy. That's what it is—jealousy. You were jealous of Emily!"

"Drop dead," she suggested. "Me, jealous of that skinny bag of bones? Can she play the violin? Jealousy? I've never heard of such a thing."

"Come off it." He chuckled in her ear. "You know damn well we're not talking about violins!"

"I'm glad to see you're enjoying all this," she said in her most prim little voice as she tried to wring seawater out of her blouse. "So, if I'm jealous of you, why are you so darn mad at me?"

"Because *you* almost drowned," he roared at her. "If you had, little Miss MacEnnaly, I—never would have spoken to you again!"

"Threats. That's all I get is threats," she snapped as she managed to work herself up on her feet, clutching desperately at the nearest bollard. "Whatever happened to care and kindness and everything like that?"

"Sooner or later everyone gets what they deserve," he said rather righteously. She shaped a fist, just in case she needed it.

"Why, you pompous old—"

"Why, you rotten kid," he interrupted as he grabbed her by the shoulders and pulled her hard up against him. "Everything's a joke with you, isn't it, Charlie MacEnnaly? Everything's funny, hey? How's this for funny?"

It was hard to kiss a girl when she couldn't stand on both feet, and Phil could feel her slipping. He broke off the kiss just in time to sweep her up in his arms again. She was looking up at him with her lovely green eyes as big as saucers. Something had just surprised her. He gave her a moment to tell, but she was silent. So, since kissing had proven so effective, he tried it again.

A soft, gentle kiss, that caressed warmly and comforted. The kind of kiss you might give to your loving niece. It wasn't enough. Her arms came around his neck and she pulled his head down. She was panting, for no good reason. When their lips touched this time there was a flash of static electricity between them. He could feel the shock register in his mind, and then run riot down his spine.

"Damn you," she muttered, and then tugged his head down again.

"And damn you too," he returned as he pressed the attack. Every inch of his body responded, and she felt it. His hand wandered down to her breast. Her blouse had long since given up the ghost. He stroked the soft firmness of her as she seemed to move toward him.

"What are you trying to do to me?" she muttered at him. Her hands came loose from his neck, and her tiny fists beat against his chest. "That's enough of that," she warned him. "I don't need any more of that—"

"You don't even know what it is," he jeered. "Talk about a textbook tootsie—you don't even know what to call it!"

"That's not true," she snapped, trying to pull away from him. "It's called a four-letter word. Lust! With a capital 'L.'"

She swung an openhanded slap at him. He tried to move away from it, and in the doing tripped over Sam and sent them both sprawling down into the water again. With all his experience he bobbed back up to the surface, pushed himself higher in the gathering darkness, and yelled. "Charlie? *Charlie*!"

"I'm right here behind you," she responded. Her hand was on the ladder, holding her safely. But for once in her life Charlie MacEnnaly didn't *want* to feel safe. She pushed off in his direction, dog-paddling madly for him, and found herself in his arms again.

"Well, hooray for you," he murmured as he held her closely. They were both ducked by an incoming wave for a second or two, and then he found the ladder and pulled them up safely.

"That was a crazy thing to do," he said. "You could have drowned. It's getting pretty dark here. I might not have found you."

"What a way to go," she said, sighing.

"What?" Phil pounded on one ear to release the pressure. All his life he had accumulated a stock of platitudes to standard questions from women. And this one was not in his book. Obviously he must have misheard her. "What was that you said?"

"Oh, Phil," she murmured, as if feeling disappointed, "I said why don't you get us back to dry land?"

Now what did I do wrong? Phil asked himself as he towed her around to the beach and pulled her ashore. Let me see, now. I said—and then she said…and then I said. Oh—! He carried her up beyond the high-water mark and helped her stretch herself out comfortably. For a brooding moment he stood over her, and then he knelt beside her.

"You know something?" he asked.

Charlie shook her head, spraying him with fine droplets that had clung in her hair.

"I'm glad I didn't marry Emily all those years ago. She bores me half to death. But you—"

"But I what?"

"But you, Charlie MacEnnaly—life in your neighborhood is always full of excitement. Did you know that?" He sat down beside her, pulling her head over into his lap, and brushed her hair away from her face.

"Only when you're around, Phil," she said softly. "Only when you're around." Silence.

"Do you suppose," he said, "that we might survive all these battles and enjoy them at the same time?"

"I don't think I could ever go back to being just a fiddle player," she confessed.

"Fiddle player?" He gave a sharp bark of laughter.

"Fiddle player," she repeated firmly.

"Then I think we ought to get married," he said.

"What a good idea," she said as she stretched in his direction. "To each other?"

"Dammit, Charlie, I'm being serious. Don't do that to me. Of course to each other. Who else could I get along so well with? Who else would take all my guff, and still take care of my pig for me?"

"Yes. There's that. But, Phil, I don't know anything at all about—well, about other things that go with marriage. Maybe we're not compatible." Anxiety struggled against her Calvinist upbringing, and Calvin was second in a two-thought race. She had a terrible sense of frustration that began in her groin and sped up to her hardened breasts. It was the sort of feeling she had never felt before.

"Not to worry," he said. "I'll teach you everything you need to know."

"When?"

"I suppose we could start now," he drawled, and then had a second thought. "I think we have a problem," he said dolefully. "Ms. Southerland. I went to drive her home and we found that the bridge was out. So she's staying overnight. And you know she's a squeaky-clean woman."

"Whose tongue is as loose as a cannon," Charlie muttered. Her stomach was bothering her. Or at least something in the area of her stomach. Maybe two aspirins will help, she told herself. Maybe I could commit suicide? I can't—wait any longer!

"I'm afraid we'll just have to wait," he said.

"Oh.... Can't we do it right here?"

He chuckled and squeezed her shoulders. "One of the things you ought to know," he advised, "is never to try it on the beach. That sand gets everywhere."

"I don't understand," she sighed. "I borrowed a book, and it doesn't say anything about sand!"

"You borrowed a book? When?" Now he was laughing outright.

"Yesterday," she admitted. "Well, it did seem that I might possibly get married some time, and I didn't want to go off to my wedding night without knowing *anything*!"

"And you weren't sure how much I knew about it all?"

"Well, how's a girl to know?" she snapped. "Maybe they ought to give men a test or something, and then they could carry a card around with them. Something like, 'The Bearer, Mr. Philip Atmor, is qualified to—to—do that thing.'" All of which brought another guffaw from Phil.

"And you needn't laugh at me," she growled. "This is practically the most important thing in a girl's life, and you laugh at me! Darn you, Philip Atmor!"

"I can't help myself," he roared. "I thought they taught all that sort of stuff in school."

"It's been a long time since you were in school," she said, her face flushed. "They teach you all of the theory and none of the practice."

"And none of the older girls talked about it?"

"What, in an episcopal orphanage? So what do we do now? And stop your laughing or I'll really hit you one!"

"Well, we've done a lot today," he told her, becoming solemn after a great deal of effort. "We managed to get rid of Emily. We managed to get engaged, didn't we?"

She nodded her head.

"And—say, what about that gay Lothario you had at your house overnight a couple of weeks ago? Where does *he* fit in?"

"James? You mean James? He's not gay. Why do you sound so suspicious?"

"Because I am. I wish you hadn't told me that the guy wasn't gay. I could put up with him if he were. Let me tell you, woman, when you get yourself engaged to me you don't need any second-team substitutes."

"Why, I do believe that *you're* jealous!" Her eyes sparkled at the thought—until she remembered her own feelings with Emily. "Maybe..." she started to say, but the fun had gone out of his face.

"I don't feel like playing any more tonight," he said grimly. "I see that you brought your car. Let's go."

It'll be all right, Charlie told herself as he drove her and her car home. We'll go into the kitchen and have a snack, and then we'll go to bed. My room has the biggest bed. I'll put on that slinky nightgown. And then he'll— But at this point Charlie's imagination ran out of information. And besides, when they reached the driveway Phil carefully deposited her at her own side door, while he and Sam wandered off into the gathering darkness, leaving her with nothing but a cool ''good night'' for her hot flashes. And that, Charlie thought, is about as bad as you can get. I think I'll have to fall back two paces and really murder the man! Or go to bed and have a good cry!

The bed won.

CHAPTER TEN

THEIR battle was reduced to armed wariness for the next several days. Sam came to join her on the second day, moving in as if he meant to stay, and taking up watch on the carpet beside her bed every night. And on that same day Charlie peered out of her window to watch Phil make a rapid approach to the end of her fence, stop, cogitate, and go back to his own house. On the next several days he repeated the same maneuver three or four times.

Charlie practiced on her violin every day, as long and as hard as her hand would allow. There was no getting off the island to escape Phil's presence. The bridge was still out of service. Her knee was back in good shape; for the first time in weeks only her heart ached. Because she intended never again to be a naive girl she scurried around for that lawyer's card which James had dropped on her. And called him.

The lawyer was suitably impressed. "Broke your finger? And then pushed you down and sprained your knee? And—what? Pushed you off the pier into the ocean when you were still crippled and he knew you couldn't swim? And maintains a pig next door to you? Lord, we can sue him for his shirt, Ms. MacEnnaly. What? You don't *want* to sue him? You just want a paper that will keep him out of your face? Yes, as easy as falling off a log. My brother is a district court clerk. I'll just get this typed up. You ought to have your restraining order by tomorrow."

"But—the bridge . . ." Charlie stuttered.

"Yes, I know about the bridge," the lawyer replied. "I'm told that some of the stringers—what? *Stringers*. The plates that hold the bridge together, under the surfacing planks. Yes, I know a nice young man with a bicycle who'd be overjoyed to attempt the crossing. Tomorrow for sure! A restraining order, Ms. MacEnnaly. Yes, a court order that prohibits him from entering your property and requires him to maintain a fifty yard distance from you at all times. On penalty of— No, ma'am. Not penalty of death— that requires a different procedure. No, this restraining order uses the old common law language. Yes. At the bottom it says 'Fail not at your peril.' He'll get a charge out of that. And a sheriff if he overlooks it."

Charlie put the phone down with a vast sigh of relief. "It's a pleasure seldom experienced," she explained to Sam, who had become a steady boarder, "to find somebody who knows what he's doing, and how to get it done. A very nice man."

Sam, coiled up on her braided rug, opened one eye in acknowledgment of a superior accomplishment, and then went back to sleep.

The paper arrived the following day, in the grimy hands of a young man about fourteen years old, full of exuberance. "Freddy," he introduced himself. "Getting over the bridge is easy. Course, it's a little greasy, but what the hey? Man workin' there says they're gonna lay down a couple of temporary planks tomorrow or the next day. Just temporary, you know. It'll make a footpath. No, ma'am, won't be able to take your car over it, but it'll be easy enough to walk across." He had gone cheerfully away, taking with him a five-dollar tip. It seemed to have been enough. He whistled as he went down the road. Some crazy tune with an African beat and unintelligible words.

Charlie lingered at the door, watching the boy pedal away. Just in time, too. She stood there with her paper in hand. Three copies, one to be served on Phil, the second to be posted on her fence, and the third to be carried with her at all times. Or so the instruction from her lawyer said. Just in time, because here came Phil on his tri-daily pilgrimage to her fence. Only this time he failed to stop!

"Hey, I've been wanting to see you," he called as he loped up to her door. "You've got Sam here?"

"Right here." And, if the battle is to be fought, let it begin here. But, just in case, she tucked the three bits of official paper behind her back. After he'd said whatever it was he had to say there would be plenty of time to post her property—and him too, she told herself.

"Sam?" The old pig stirred not a muscle at his master's call.

"Your visit is wasted," she said coldly. "If that's what you came over for. Your pig has decided to join up with the good guys."

"That's what I came for too," he said. "To join up with the good guys. I'm sorry, Charlie, that I was such a grumpy damn bore up at the bridge a couple of nights ago. I really didn't mean it. I just—well, I hated to hear about that guy you were dating."

"James?"

"Yeah, that guy. I hope you'll forgive me, because I..." A long hesitation. He looked like the condemned man when the executioner first put his hand to the gallows lever. A dry swallow, and he started again. "Because I love you, Charlie MacEnnaly."

"My ears," she said, "are truly deceiving me. I thought you said—"

"I had trouble with *my* ears just the other day," he said. "Same thing. What you heard me say is I love you, Charlie. L-U-V! Love!"

"I—think you may be misspelling it," she said, "but I take the meaning." And she started to cry.

"What the hell have I done wrong now?" Perplexity brought on a frown, and the frown brought on furrows. She hated to see Phil with furrows. It made him look forty-four instead of thirty-four.

"You haven't done anything wrong," she hastened to assure him. "I'm crying because I'm happy."

"Ah," he said, as perplexed as ever. "You're happy? Of course, happy tears."

"One of your many faults, Philip Atmor," she said in a determined voice, "is that you talk too much. Kiss me."

"The very thought," he sighed. "And I should have thought of it myself." And so he did. Both thought and kissed.

"Manna from heaven," she told Sam a few minutes later. She was just about caught up with her breathing. Her spine still tingled with the shock of it all, and for some reason her stomach was upset again. Damn the man, she told herself, and wished he would do it again—quickly. But, rather than stay around to observe the effect, Phil had set her down flat-footed and made a dash for his own house.

And when he came back again, and she had regained her normally cool temperament, he brought out a little blue jewelry box, and when she opened the box there lay a simple solitaire diamond mounted on a platinum ring, which, when she stopped fumbling, just fitted the third finger on her left hand.

Charlie, completely out of breath, plumped herself down on the couch and began to cry again. And Ms. Southerland, who had come over to observe, gave everybody a big smile and then joined Charlie in the tears.

"Happy tears. I hope," Phil told his pig and swore for years afterward that there were tears in Sam's eyes too! But Charlie was not entirely bereft of reason. The restraining order was burning a hole in her pocket. She would have liked to destroy it—but, she told herself, this romance is so off-and-on that maybe I'd better keep it. I might need it later. So, moving slowly so as not to call anyone's attention to what she was doing, she tucked the three copies of that official Command from the Commonwealth of Massachusetts down under the cushions of the couch. And cried some more.

When Phil and Charlie, along with Sam, finally made their way over to the city, where Atmor Fisheries had its headquarters, Claudia Sylvia was somewhat overwhelmed by the story. Things were going faster than she had anticipated. And there was no doubt about it, Charlie MacEnnaly was a wonderful girl, just right for her Philip. So much so that she turned on her boss and said, "Go out in the plant and boss something. Charlie and I have a few woman things to talk over." He went without a single protest.

"He's a good lad," Claudia said as she dabbed at a loose tear near the end of her nose. "It broke him up considerably when his mother ran off with some local idiot. And then his father—died. And with all that grief piled on his shoulders Phil had to put his shoulder to the wheel. The company almost went bankrupt. And then that foolish woman—Emily something-or-other . . . the one he planned to marry? When she found out that the money was all gone, then wham, she was gone too. So Phil went to work. Worked days and went to Harvard University night school. Pulled us up by the heels, he did, worked himself to the bone, and never had a minute for running around." And why should I say a word about his three-day-a-week partying? Claudia told herself.

"I didn't know," Charlie gasped. "All that? He seemed so—lonely. Even in the middle of a crowd he was lonely."

"And, during the thirteen years that followed, he has kept his nose to the grindstone, and his mind on the goal. Always."

"Yes, I'm sure he has," Charlie replied. "Of course, I've been his next-door neighbor for months." Claudia was seized with a coughing fit, and blushed prettily. "But what I don't understand is why you are telling me all this."

"Because I want you and my boy to have a fine life," Claudia said. "I rather suspect that Phil knows a great deal about women. To be honest about it, Charlie—I may call you Charlie?" Charlotte Mac-Ennaly nodded her head in agreement. "Well, then— Charlie—I often think that beneath Phil's soft innocent exterior there beats the heart of a first-class pirate. Just watch your step, girl. Watch your step!"

"He'd better know a lot about women," Charlie whispered. "I don't know *anything* about men! I bought a book about marriage and all that. No pictures, though."

"Never mind that," Claudia told her. "Just go by your intuition, love. But watch out. When that innocent little look shows up, he's up to something."

That was the moment that Phil chose to come back in, whistling. "Did you ladies have a good talk?"

"You'd better believe it," Charlie said. "Your mother and I have—I mean, your—I mean, Claudia and I had a good talk, all about you. Were your ears burning?"

"You were right the first time." He hugged Claudia. "This *is* my mother, for sure." And then he went across the room and put an arm around Charlie. "Are we ever going to make her a grandmother?"

"Why—I don't know," Charlie gasped. "That's supposed to be something we talk about in the dark of night, after we can't find anything else to do. And—look out!" Her voice rose from a sweet contralto to a pitch somewhere between squeal and scream. Sam, brought to attention by the noise, rushed the new intruder, a man of medium height, dressed in his stylish best, and wearing a hat. And Phil was charging across the room looking to do murder.

There was only one thing Charlie could do. She thrust out one of her legs directly in front of Phil, and in a magic moment the charging bull did a head-over-tail roll and whacked his head into the wainscoting.

"Over here, James." Charlie staggered to her feet. "Get over here before the wild man wakes up again. He thinks you're making out with his girl."

"What a happy thought," her agent said bravely, but he hurried all the same, across the room and up behind Charlie, with a chair to right and left to protect his flanks. "And how did you get along with my brother the lawyer?"

"Shut up, idiot. Do you want to get yourself massacred?"

"Ah. One of those types?"

"Two of those types, and he's getting up."

"Er—Mr. Atmor," James stammered. "I fail to see why you would worry about a girl I have known since she was five years old."

"I'm gonna wring your neck," Phil muttered.

"Take your hat off, James. Now!" Puzzled, James did as he was instructed.

"Dear me," Claudia said, studying the fringe of white hair that surrounded James's bald spot.

"For cryin' out loud," Phil said. "He's from the rocking-chair brigade! What the hell were you doing with this—gay Lothario?"

"Nothing," Charlie hurried to say. "What could I be doing? Setting up my own geriatric ward? James is my agent. Got it? Agent."

"I don't intend to stand still for this nonsense," James said, aggrieved. "You have no right to go around in public questioning my sexual preferences!"

"He was only quoting. Something from *The Fair Penitent*. Go home, James," Charlie hissed at him. "While you're able, go home!"

"Ah—well," James muttered. "A quotation? Nothing wrong with a quotation." And he ducked out of the room.

"And don't come back," Phil yelled down the hall at the back of him.

"Dear Lord, not you too," Charlie sighed. "I need an agent for when I go back to work."

"You're through going back to work," Phil stated bluntly.

"Just like that?"

"Just like that," he said, looming over her with dark flashing eyes, as if he were prepared to make a human sacrifice. "Just like that! Do I hear any objections?'' A delicious little chill spread over Charlie, and ran down all her nerves.

"No. No objections," she squeaked very meekly. He looked down at her, astonished. And well you ought to be astonished, Charlie told herself. I know one thing about this *girl*. If he thinks, after fifteen years of practice, I'm going to quit the violin just because he *orders* it, boy, what a surprise he's going to get.

"I've got several more things to check up on," he said. "Charlie, you sit there until I come back. You hear?"

"Yes," she said, and then, since that failed to sound subservient enough, "yes, sir." Phil stomped down the hall looking for somebody to bite. The staff of Atmor Fisheries scattered to the winds to keep out of his way.

"Was that wise?" Claudia asked gently. "You're going to give up the violin?"

"You wouldn't want me to disobey my loving husband, would you?" Charlie asked, grinning. "At least not in the first thirty days. I'm looking forward to this marriage business. So I told him what he wanted to hear. I'll have my innings later."

"That's the spirit, girl. I don't want Phil to marry a doormat."

"Have no fear, Mother Claudia," Charlie said, and the twinkle was back in her calculating green eyes. "I want to marry him because I'm mad about him. I wish I knew exactly why *he* wants to marry *me*."

"I wouldn't be surprised if it wasn't for exactly the same reason."

"If that's the case," Charlie said, "you've heard our last argument."

"I doubt that very much," Claudia said, chuckling. "And, just in case it doesn't work out the way you think, let me repeat for you one of my grandmother's favorites. Don't ever go to sleep on an argument. Always settle up before your last cuddle every night." It was wise advice, Charlie thought, lost in another daydream about the subject.

That was the moment that young Alice Sturdevent, the apprentice secretary in Phil's outer office, barged in. "Just back from lunch, Ms. Sylvia," the child trilled. "They've got a great lobster salad up at the Counting House. Why don't you go for *your* lunch? Oh! I didn't think you had company."

"You'll have to meet her some time," Claudia sighed. "Charlotte, this is Alice Sturdevent. She works in our office. Alice, this is Charlotte MacEnnaly, the famous violinist."

Little Alice's eyes sparkled with an overabundance of enthusiasm, and hardly a thimbleful of caution. "Ms. MacEnnaly? Are you arranging the wedding?"

"Why, yes," Charlie said. "Everybody seems to know more than I do about the whole thing. How did you learn?"

"Shut up, Alice, and go away!" Claudia, feeling the ground shake beneath her feet, did her best to bluster. But Charlie had pinned the girl down with her own hypnotic eye.

"How did you know?" she asked softly.

"Oh, everybody knows about it," Alice said nervously. "They've even set up a betting pool down in the shop. You know?"

"No, I don't know," Charlie returned pleasantly. "What's it all about?"

Claudia Sylvia was about to die of apoplexy. Even little Alice realized that she was walking, dragging one foot in the quicksand. She bailed out all her information in one quick breath. "Oh, I was here when Ms. Sylvia told Mr. Atmor—she said, 'If you really want to punish that woman you'll have to marry her'! Honest, Ms. MacEnnaly, I really didn't mean to blab it all over the office, and—" More tears came to shut down the conversation.

"And what did *he* say?" she asked the girl.

Alice dug up a Kleenex and managed to cut off the flood. "I don't know," the girl muttered. "Somebody came in for something and I didn't hear any more, but he must have decided to try it, mustn't he? He *is* going to marry you, isn't he?"

"I think, Alice, you've said enough," Claudia commented. "Go out to the ladies' room and clean yourself up. No, better still, you'd better take the rest of the afternoon off. And hurry. Before he comes back and kills us all!"

"Well, he *is* going to marry you," the girl muttered as she rushed down the hall. Charlie leaned back in her chair and stared out of the window. A fog was closing in. Probably in another three hours the harbor would be blanketed completely. *Is* he going to marry me? she thought. More than likely I'll hand him his head on a plate. She started to get up.

"He said stay," Claudia murmured. "It was only a little office joke, Charlie. We didn't even know what you looked like back in those days. Don't, please. Don't go! It's all my fault!"

"Sure it is—and Sam's too, I suppose." Charlie stood up on a weak pair of knees. "Coming, Sam?" Her faithful—and his no longer faithful—pigperson gradually cantilevered himself up onto his knees and padded out behind her. Charlie stalked down the stairs, and out on to South First Street, with Sam close behind her. Any waterfront area was difficult for a slight but beautiful woman alone. Charlie received tour different propositions in the first block. One of them was even decent. A snarl or a squeal from Sam was enough to discourage any further attempts.

There was a small but growing traffic jam ahead of her, just at the entrance of the city's parking garages. Walking swiftly, head down, she caught up with the head of the column just as Phil caught up with her!

"Charlie!" His hand on her shoulder turned her around to face him. "What the hell are we into now?"

She caught her breath. Thunder clouded his forehead, and yet he was so—beautiful—that she had no answer for him.

"Well?"

She licked her dry lips, stared at him for a moment and then recalled the words. "If you really want to punish that woman you'll have to marry her," she said, so softly that they could barely be heard over the noises of the car engines. "And I wish you wouldn't curse so much, Mr. Atmor."

"Whoever told you a crazy thing like that?"

"Your secretary," she said primly. "And Alice, that nice little girl who works in your office. Did you think I could make up something like that?"

"I think you could have dreamed up almost anything," he snapped. "But, whatever excuse you have, it's not going to work. Listen up, Charlotte MacEnnaly." He stabbed at her with his forefinger, making a bruise or two on her shoulder. "You—and I—are going—to—marry. Got it?"

"The hell we are," she replied with enthusiasm. "Why would I want to marry a barbarian who hates me, who wants to punish me by marriage, who broke my finger, who sprained my knee, who just bruised my shoulder? Who would be that stupid?"

"Bruised your shoulder?"

"Bruised my shoulder. Look!" She unbuttoned her blouse and slipped it off her shoulder so he could see, forgetting completely where they were. A half-dozen horns blew, and more drivers than that rolled down their windows and applauded.

He glared at her and pulled her blouse back up. "That's what you get for knowing a guy like me," he yelled at her. "You could be arrested for indecent exposure. And it's not ladylike to curse like that!"

"Ladylike?" she bellowed at him. "You wouldn't know a lady if she came along and bit you. Now turn me loose, you—you monster!"

"Turn you loose? Never a chance," he yelled back at her. "We're going to get married. Right now. Come along." He took her wrist and started to tow her back down the street to where his car was parked.

"I wouldn't go around the corner with you," she muttered as she dug her heels in.

"That's it," he declared. "That's the very end. Now shut up, Charlie, and come with me."

"You can't make me," she told him. And he proceeded to demonstrate that he could. With one swooping grab he threw her over his shoulder, with her head hanging downward against his back in a fireman's lift. At first the shock kept her quiet. As he started to walk up the street with her over his shoulder the crowd whistled and applauded. It was enough to ignite her. She struggled and kicked and cursed him with all the strength in her, to absolutely no effect. He tightened his grip on her legs and strode casually along the pavement, whistling.

Charlie had so worn herself out that when he unlocked his car door she gave up the struggle. "Are you coming quietly?" he asked.

"Yes," she said. "But I'll hate you for the rest of your life."

"Good," he snapped as he dumped her into the back seat. "You can have fun explaining it to our children." Sam managed to climb in behind her. Phil slammed the door behind them. It was no use struggling at that point. She knew that the back doors locked when the door closed, and could only be opened by a button on the dashboard.

For a moment, as he walked around the car, she thought to jump over the seats and lock *him* out, but hesitation spoiled her attempt. She slumped back on the seat, raging in fury. He started the engine and moved out into the traffic.

"Where are you taking me?" she snarled. "Kidnapping me," she amended.

"I'm taking you home," he snapped. "And then—"

"I know," she growled, "you're going to rape me."

"I'm going to marry you," he snapped. "After that—well, who knows?"

Charlie settled back in her seat. If glowering eyes were a lethal weapon he would have had a hole in the back of his head long before they reached the bridge to Fairhaven. He turned the rearview mirror so he could watch her, and then paid attention to his driving, whistling all the way.

Sam managed to wiggle himself up on the back seat, and moved over to nuzzle her cheek. She put an arm around her pet and lay her head against his shoulder. "Except for you, Sam, I'd like to kill all the male creatures in the world." Said loudly enough to be heard in the front seat, of course.

"Good idea," Phil replied. "Now please shut up. I'm having trouble remembering this song." Back to the whistling.

"Oh, is that a song? I thought you were coughing. You can't whistle worth a nickel, Phil Atmor."

"Thank you, Charlie," he replied. "That's the nicest thing you've said to me all afternoon."

Phil parked his rental car on the near side of the bridge and helped them all out. "They've put a narrow plank across," he pointed out. "Good enough for walking—if we're careful."

"I pay my taxes regularly," she snapped. "How long do I have to wait for the bridge to be repaired?"

"About two years," he said. "Are you walking?"

"On that narrow thing? Not me! You've got the wrong girl."

"Okay," he said wearily, and tossed her up and over his shoulder again.

"Don't—don't you—"

"Dare?" he interrupted. "Look down at the water, Charlotte. See how narrow that plank is. If you don't quit that struggling I'm going to slip and we'll both fall into the river. Of course, I can swim. How about you?"

"All right," she muttered, and stopped her fighting. When he set foot on dry land he stopped. "Are you walking, or riding?" he asked. "We're going up to the house, no matter what."

A thoroughly subdued Charlie muttered, "I'll walk." She had trouble finding her land legs when he set her down. She locked on to his arm to steady herself. "All right, I'm ready," she said.

"Go on up to the house," he told her. She started out, still not quite sure that her legs would hold her. Sam crowded her side, keeping her on a straight path. At the top of the incline she sensed that something was missing. She stopped and turned around. Phil was still down at the bridge, hauling at the end of the plank walk. He pulled it all the way off the bridge, slammed it down on the shore, and started up the hill beside her, whistling as he went.

"Why you—rotten..." she gasped. "You know darn well I can't lift that plank, you—"

"That's right, you can't," he chuckled. "And, as I recall, you can't swim either. Tough luck, Charlie."

"Lord," she muttered, "And I was going to confess everything."

"Confess what?"

"I wouldn't tell you now if my life—"

"Depended on it," he interrupted. "And it does. Tell me."

"Don't think you can terrorize me, Phil Atmor!" He took a step in her direction. "All right," she half screamed. "All right." She took a deep breath to settle her nerves. "Emily didn't run away. I frightened her off by telling her that you broke my hand and my knee in a fit of anger—and when you barked at her she ran. So there."

"So there," he said, chuckling. "Stick your tongue out, Charlie. That was good work. I've been trying to discourage for a long time! I guess I was being too gentle."

There was a musty smell inside the house. Charlotte followed her usual routine, moving around to open all the windows talking to herself. Phil disappeared into the kitchen. In a few minutes the delightful smell of omelet filled the air. She realized that it had been a long time since breakfast, and walked out to join him.

"I thought you could only cook a couple of things. What is it?"

"A western omelet," he said. "I went to a western omelet cooking school once, but could only master one recipe. This is it. Ready to eat?"

"I'm starved," Charlie said as she pulled out a chair. Her anger had gone—drifted away on the shore breezes. And yet she recalled exactly how everything had happened. All those months of arguement, followed by the sweetness of making up. And you promised to marry the man, for goodness' sake, she told herself. Some people are slightly off key; people like me are plain stupid! Never fall asleep on an argument. Making up can be fun, fun, fun!

"Here you are." He called her back from her dreamland as he placed a full plate in front of her. "Tea? Coffee?"

"Milk," she said. And for once caught that little smile that tugged at the corners of his mouth.

The omelet was good, the milk sweet, and the man was—lovable? Perhaps, she thought as she cleaned her plate. But is that enough for us to live on for all our lives?

Evidently he was having the same sort of debate with himself. When the meal was finished he cleared the plates off the table and sat down again, placing his hand over hers. "It's five o'clock, Charlie. And it's make or break time. At exactly six o'clock I'm going to ask you one question, no more. From now until six I want you to think about us—you and I—a pair. Got that?"

"What will *you* be doing while I'm thinking?" she enquired.

"I'll be going down to the river and putting the planks back on the bridge."

"And?"

"And, from now until six, if you think for any reason that you don't want to hear my question, or you don't want to answer it, you're free to go down and cross the bridge. The car on the other side is a rental. The keys are hanging on the hook by the side door. Take them all, if that's your decision, and go with my blessings."

"What—what do *you* feel about my going?"

"I don't want you to go," he said, and she could see the hurt hiding behind his eyes.

"I'll think about it," she promised.

Phil snapped his fingers at Sam, who, surprisingly, elected to go with him down to the river. The planking was heavier to restore than it had been to remove. He sweated at it for a half hour before working it back so that the bridge could be crossed. As he stood up to stretch his aching back muscles he felt a soft hand on his bare shoulder, and turned around. Charlie was there behind him, a lovely smile on her face.

"I don't need any more time to think," she said softly.

"Oh?" He didn't know whether to laugh or frown. If she had needed only a half hour she was very sure of herself. Perhaps it wouldn't be wise to ask? At that moment a limousine drove up to the opposite side of the bridge, and a group of people began to climb out.

Sink or swim, he told himself, and then he crossed fingers on both hands behind his back.

"Charlie?" he asked. She had been watching him carefully.

"Yes?"

"Charlie, I love you. Will you marry me?" The words tumbled out in wild confusion, like water breaking through a dam. "Will you?"

"Of course I will," she answered. "I don't know any woman in the world who could turn down such a bargain!" She was on top of him before he could comprehend the answer, throwing her arms around his neck, kissing him hungrily.

"Oh," he said stupidly. And then "Oh?" And then, with a yell of delight, "Oh!" They were deep in the wildness of another kiss when the party on the other side of the river began to cross, one at a time, carefully. He broke their kiss with reluctance, setting Charlie down a step or two away from him.

"Darling," he said, "I want you to meet the Reverend Ostermil, from the episcopal Church."

"Why, you dirty rat," she said, but she was all smiles as she said it. "You planned this all the time, didn't you?"

"That I did," he chuckled. "That I did."

"It was a fine wedding," she said after the guests had gone. "And to have Claudia and Ms. Southerland for my bridesmaids was a stroke of genius. But whatever in the world made you pick James for the best man?"

"Because I wanted him to suffer," he said, chuckling. "I wanted to have him stand there and look at how beautiful you were, and to know he couldn't have you! In addition, he was the only man left in the office when I told Claudia to round up a crowd!"

"My feet hurt," Charlie said. She sat down on the couch in the middle of the thoroughly littered living room, and slipped her feet out of her pumps. "And now we're all alone."

His ear was tuned for the little trembling sound in her voice. He walked over to the end table by the window with a package. "I bought you a gift," he said. "Why don't you open it while I step out for a minute?"

"All right," she replied sadly, "but I was so—rushed I didn't have a chance to get you a gift."

"Yes, you did," he replied very solemnly. "Open your package. I'll be right back."

She watched him go, admiring the strength of him, the wonderfully facile face, the curl of his hair just below the nape of his neck. And when the door closed behind him she unwrapped the book.

What Every Girl Needs, the title said, *Or What To Do On Your Wedding Night*. Why, that marvelously foolish man, she told herself as she gazed out into space. As if any woman needed that much instruction. With a wisp of a smile on her face she opened the book. It contained two hundred blank pages, but there was something written in pencil on the front page. It wasn't exactly a message, but rather a schedule. It said this:

Go upstairs and take a shower.
Lay out a warm nightgown on the foot of the bed
in case of fire.
Climb in bed and take a deep breath.

"Oh, that crazy man," she said. "Come on, Sam."
Up the stairs they paraded. She was barely out of the
bathroom when she heard him running up the stairs
and directly into the shower. Sam took up his regular
guard post on the rug beside her bed, and curled up
for sleep. Charlie fidgeted. She had no idea what to
wear. Most of her clothes were still in her own house.
She opened the wardrobe labeled "Hers." Hanging on
the single hanger was one of his massive white shirts.
Hurrying now, apprehensive, she snatched it off the
hanger and laid it down at the foot of the bed. Nude,
she stood before her window and quickly brushed her
hair. It seemed foolish to put on makeup, but just a
touch of perfume? And then into bed, shivering, although the sheets were warm. The bedroom door
opened, and Phil came in, his hair still wet from the
shower, a short robe wrapped around his waist.

"What did you have to go out for?" she asked.

"To take the planks back off the bridge," he said.
"We don't want any visitors tomorrow. Do we?"

"I—I don't know the custom," she half whispered. "I didn't get you a gift. I—Phil, I don't know
anything more about getting married than just this.
I—hope you won't be disappointed."

"I won't be," he chuckled. "You're my gift, and I'll
show you all you need to know, love. But first—I'm

not much for operating in my bedroom as a spectator sport. Sam?"

The little pig opened one eye.

"Sam." He prodded the animal with one of his bare toes. Sam made no attempt to move.

"Dammit, Sam! I can't wait any longer!" Impatient, Charlie told herself as she shifted over to the far side of the bed. So am I!

"Sam?" One last appeal, and then, "I knew I should have bought a dog."

At this terrible insult the magnificent little pig got up, and started slowly for the door. Phil followed him, urging him along with one bare foot. At the threshold Sam sat down stubbornly and squealed an objection.

"Oh, the poor little fellow," Charlie said as she watched her husband pick up the sixty-five pounds of rotund little pig and deposit him gently on the carpet in the hall. Sam groaned as if his heart were broken.

Phil looked down at him for just a compassionate second. "Say good night, Sam," he said, and slammed the door between them. Sam could hear the complaining of the bedsprings behind the door as his master did a racing dive under the sheets, and the squealing laughter of his new mistress as she received him. Deciding his day was definitely finished, Sam circled himself a couple of times, and lay down on the rug. Sleep was impossible; there was too much noise coming from the bedroom behind him.

Share the adventure—and the romance—of

HARLEQUIN 🎗 PRESENTS®

A Year
DOWN UNDER

If you missed any titles in this miniseries,
here's your chance to order them:

Harlequin Presents®—A Year Down Under

#11519	HEART OF THE OUTBACK by Emma Darcy	$2.89	❑
#11527	NO GENTLE SEDUCTION by Helen Bianchin	$2.89	❑
#11537	THE GOLDEN MASK by Robyn Donald	$2.89	❑
#11546	A DANGEROUS LOVER by Lindsay Armstrong	$2.89	❑
#11554	SECRET ADMIRER by Susan Napier	$2.89	❑
#11562	OUTBACK MAN by Miranda Lee	$2.99	❑
#11570	NO RISKS, NO PRIZES by Emma Darcy	$2.99	❑
#11577	THE STONE PRINCESS by Robyn Donald	$2.99	❑
#11586	AND THEN CAME MORNING by Daphne Clair	$2.99	❑
#11595	WINTER OF DREAMS by Susan Napier	$2.99	❑
#11601	RELUCTANT CAPTIVE by Helen Bianchin	$2.99	❑
#11611	SUCH DARK MAGIC by Robyn Donald	$2.99	❑
	(limited quantities available on certain titles)		

TOTAL AMOUNT	$
POSTAGE & HANDLING	$
($1.00 for one book, 50¢ for each additional)	
APPLICABLE TAXES*	$ _____
TOTAL PAYABLE	$ _____
(check or money order—please do not send cash)	

To order, complete this form and send it, along with a check or money order for the
total above, payable to Harlequin Books, to: *In the U.S.*: 3010 Walden Avenue,
P.O. Box 9047, Buffalo, NY 14269-9047; *In Canada*: P.O. Box 613, Fort Erie, Ontario,
L2A 5X3.

Name: _____

Address: _____ City: _____

State/Prov.: _____ Zip/Postal Code: _____

*New York residents remit applicable sales taxes.
Canadian residents remit applicable GST and provincial taxes.   YDUF

POSTCARDS FROM EUROPE

HARLEQUIN PRESENTS®

Hi!
Spending a year in Europe. You won't believe how great the men are! Will be visiting Greece, Italy, France and more.
Wish you were here—how about joining us in January?

There's a handsome Greek just waiting to meet you.

THE ALPHA MAN
by Kay Thorpe

Harlequin Presents #1619

Available in January wherever Harlequin books are sold.

HPPFEG

Relive the romance...
Harlequin® is proud to bring you

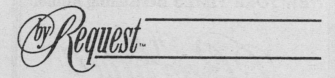
by Request™

A new collection of three complete novels every month. By the most requested authors, featuring the most requested themes.

Available in January:

WESTERN LOVING

They're ranchers, horse trainers, cowboys...
They're willing to risk their lives.
But are they willing to risk their hearts?

Three complete novels in one special collection:

RISKY PLEASURE by JoAnn Ross
VOWS OF THE HEART by Susan Fox
BY SPECIAL REQUEST by Barbara Kaye

Available wherever Harlequin books are sold.

NEW YORK TIMES **Bestselling Author**

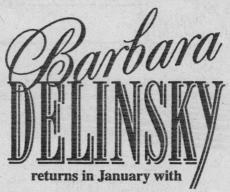

Barbara DELINSKY

returns in January with

THE REAL THING

Stranded on an island off the coast of Maine,
Deirdre Joyce and Neil Hersey got the
solitude they so desperately craved—
but they also got each other, something they
hadn't expected. Nor had they expected
to be consumed by a desire so powerful
that the idea of living alone again was
unimaginable. A marrige of "convenience"
made sense—or did it?

B0B7

 HARLEQUIN®

Harlequin® Historical

FLASH: ROMANCE MAKES HISTORY!

History the Harlequin way, that is. Our books invite you to experience a past you never read about in grammar school!

Travel back in time with us, and pirates will sweep you off your feet, cowboys will capture your heart, and noblemen will lead you to intrigue and romance, *always* romance—because that's what makes each Harlequin Historical title a thrilling escape for you, four times every month. Just think of the adventures you'll have!

So pick up a Harlequin Historical novel today, and relive history in your wildest dreams....

Fifty red-blooded, white-hot, true-blue hunks
from every State in the Union!

Look for MEN MADE IN AMERICA! Written by some
of our most poplar authors, these stories feature fifty of
the strongest, sexiest men, each from a different state in
the union!

Two titles available every other month at your favorite
retail outlet.

In January, look for:

DREAM COME TRUE by Ann Major (Florida)
WAY OF THE WILLOW by Linda Shaw (Georgia)

In March, look for:

TANGLED LIES by Anne Stuart (Hawaii)
ROGUE'S VALLEY by Kathleen Creighton (Idaho)

You won't be able to resist MEN MADE IN AMERICA!